SEASONED

BY

FIRE

Randy Loubier

This book is a work of fiction. Any resemblance to real persons is a coincidence.

ISBN: 979-8-9861527-6-9

DEDICATION

To the people of Japan: May you rediscover the source of your fire.

TABLE OF CONTENTS

Every Ship Has a Captain

Every ship has a captain," his brother had said.

That statement rolled through his mind like the waves on the Sea of Japan. At 45, Kai Oda was back at the helm. Sailing had never been a hobby or career for Kai. It was a way of life. The water, his ship, and the crew he captained were as much a part of his identity as Kai's long hair and beard.

With both hands on the ship's wheel, Kai smiled to himself and tilted his head back to witness the Creator's glorious night sky. This voyage was different than any he had ventured.

Foreign trade had been lucrative for Kai. He had amassed enough wealth for many lifetimes. But a year ago, he knew he was missing something from his life. Many things were missing, perhaps. He'd never been married or had a family—the sea had been his mistress since adulthood.

Kai's first name was Nobukai, though nobody knew him by that name. He was named in the tradition of the father he never met, Oda Nobunaga. By 1582, his father had lived a legendary life as a famous samurai and Shogun, but he cut it short while Kai was still in the womb. Seppuku (Japanese ritual suicide) was an honorable death, but it left Kai with just a myth of a father, and an estranged, depressed mother, Lady No.

1

Nobukai's childhood was privileged but distant. His siblings were much older, the nearest in age to him was twenty-eight years older. Therefore, they were disinterested in him, and perhaps worse, Kai wondered if they thought he was the cause of their father's death. Lady No, never a maternal woman, was even less of a mother to Kai.

It was not surprising when, at the age of fifteen, Kai left home and married the Sea of Japan. He found a ship that would hire him and never returned to land for more than a few weeks at a time.

That is, until a year ago.

Kai's attention shifted towards the night sky to the south. Within a few moments, he noticed three strikes of lightning. They lit up the sky just enough that he could catch the storm clouds rolling in. When they had set sail for their five-day journey earlier that day, the weather was fair, but he could tell rain was lurking.

Kai's second in command, Enji, approached the captain from behind. They had spent the better half of their careers sailing together. They made so many trips to China and Korea that they might have listed the Sea of Japan as their place of residence. However, they were much more than just shipmates and business partners. They had become best friends after decades of sailing the seas together. They knew each other like an old married couple.

Enji could tell from Kai's posture—back straight as a board, both arms at a 90-degree angle, hands firmly attached to the ship's wheel—that the captain was deep in thought.

Enji broke the silence. "Are you seeing what I'm seeing? Looks like a storm is brewing in the distance. I'll give it 30 minutes before the rain starts blowing."

Kai thought for a few seconds before responding. He had spent the last fourteen months with his brother Nobumasa at his remote cabin in the northern mountains of Japan. Fourteen months away from the ocean! That was Kai's most extended absence from his first love since he was a boy.

Now, hours into his first voyage back at sea, he watched the storm blow in as he had countless times before. But this storm felt new, exciting, and prophetic.

"Imagine that," he responded to Enji. "My first voyage in over a year, and the Creator decides to display His masterly work of art. Just look at how He lights up the sky in the dark of the night."

Enji stepped forward to be shoulder to shoulder with Kai. Just then, a gust of wind swept across the ship's deck, and several lightning bolts appeared in the sky. Booming sounds of thunder followed the lightning.

A second gust of wind smacked against the two men, letting them know they were heading for rough sailing.

Enji spoke loudly over the gusts, "I'll get the men to take a couple of sails down and prepare for the storm."

"Thank you," Kai responded.

Kai's heart beat a little faster. Not out of fear. With his experience, a storm made sailing more of a challenge and a responsibility for the lives of others. Kai had spent his adult life mastering his skills. He embraced the test that awaited him.

Growing up, Kai was closest to Nobumasa in age and relationship. Nobumasa, though twenty-eight years older, lived at home with Kai. He was kind, quiet, studious and had a peaceful, contented personality. Nobumasa met a Christian missionary at the age of 41 and converted.

Being a Christian in Japan, however, was dangerous. Since 1549 when the first missionaries landed in Japan, many people loved the religion, but most distrusted it as a front for foreign imperialism. By 1595 when Nobumasa converted, it was a scandal for the family of the former Shogun.

That year, Kai was thirteen years old when he watched as his brother was sent away for being a Christian; it was the last time he saw him. Nobumasa was escorted 1000 miles to a remote mountain in Aomori-ken. He was given some supplies and tools and left to survive alone.

Over the past thirty years, Kai occasionally sailed in and out of the port of Aomori, Japan. Each time, he would think of his brother and wonder if he was still living in the mountains nearby. In 1626, at 44, Kai decided to find out.

Within sixty seconds, the entire crew was on deck, busy at work. It was considered an honor to be part of Kai's crew. He was not only known as a great sailor but also one of the best overseas traders in Japan. Kai had the reputation of getting top dollar for any goods he was trading, meaning more profit for his crew. Everyone in the industry respected him. His staff knew he would pay them well. Other traders knew Kai always had the best product available.

The crew hurried across the ship's deck. They took down sails, trimmed the others, and readied the deck for rough seas. Kai couldn't tell what was moving faster, his crew or the oncoming storm. Bolts of lightning flashed dramatically, and the sound of thunder was louder than the howling wind. The shipmates' activity was precise and practiced. They knew the drills, what must happen in the proper order, how many hands it would take to finish each task expeditiously, and when to check back in with Enji.

It had taken some effort, but Kai found his brother, Nobumasa. The reunion was joyous and life-altering. Living as a hermit, Nobumasa had not only survived but was happy. The first couple of years had been burdensome, indeed, life-threatening. But he built log structures, fireplaces, and animal pens over time. He trapped for fur, traded them in Hirosaki, and generally found a rhythm in the seasons. It was him and his Creator, living together in harmony.

Nobumasa knew firsthand the risks of living in a hostile anti-Christian environment. But he also knew the joy of knowing his Creator personally. This dichotomy became a passion for him. The fundamental question he continuously put before God was, "How can I help the Japanese know the joy you have for us, even though they erroneously think you are a foreign God?"

Over the years of solitary living, Nobumasa developed an Asian method of studying the Bible. As Nobumasa understood it, the Bible claimed that the benevolent uncreated Creator had created the Japanese, loved the Japanese, and revealed Himself to them. Even the ancient Japanese manuscripts, the Kojiki and Nihon Shoki, claimed the same, yet the Japanese people refused to worship their Creator because the Christians had come from imperialist countries. Nobumasa and the Japanese people, understandably, refused imperialism. But in the turmoil, most Japanese people rejected their Creator, too.

Therefore, Nobumasa was compelled to help bridge the gap of understanding for the nation of Japan. He developed the Tea Room Scrolls to teach the fundamentals of Christ *in secret*. What appeared to the outsider to be a secular tearoom was a private classroom in which the students discovered the joy of Jesus.

Kai spent all fourteen months learning the Bible using the Tea Room Scrolls method. It changed his perspective, and he found the joy his brother told him he would. The scripture proved true, Kai's mind was renewed, and his spirit was regenerated.

As Kai continued his studies at the Oda Onsen tearoom, he knew he needed to bring the scrolls to Asia. He resolved to convince his brother.

Nobumasa agreed to let Kai carry the scrolls abroad. While the scrolls were designed for the Japanese people, Nobumasa had already prophesied that Japan would be a slow brewing tea, continuing to reject their Creator long into the future. He said God had special timing for the Japanese nation. God would give the Japanese the perseverance to hold His values of wa, purity, knowing one's place, and giri. But at a particular time in history, Japan would not only explode with faith; it would lead the world back to His values.

Now, as Kai watched the storm batter his ship, he felt a special anointing on him and his mission. Part of the mission was to find alpine tea plants in China that would grow well in the northern mountains of Japan. Kai's brother had a keen interest in tea. His Japanese tea ceremonies were important in celebrating his faith, and he wanted a tea that was unique to his land. But he had not been able to overcome the challenge of growing a ceremonial grade tea in the cold salt sprayed mountains of northern Honshu, Japan.

So, while one part of his mission was importing tea plants to Japan, the second part of Kai's mission was on what he was exporting from Japan: the Tea Room Scrolls.

Kai was burning with a passion and purpose unlike any other time in his life. His earthly father was a legend in unifying Japan politically, but Kai was now living for something of even greater significance to Japan.

Kai called his crew together on the bridge of the ship.

"Circle around for just a minute, men," Kai said to his crew. "I realize not all of you share my faith and belief in the Creator of the Universe, but with my first trip back on the water and this storm quickly approaching, I would like to pray over us and our ship as we head into the unknown. So, please bow your heads and close your eyes with me for just a second."

Several of the men quickly shifted their attention towards Enji. The second in command gave a slight nod in approval to the others of what their captain asked.

"Heavenly Father," Kai began. "Thank you for the opportunity you have blessed us with to prosper on this voyage. Prepare our way and bless our ventures when we land in China. Protect our crew, be our comfort and confidence. Let your will be done in all that we do. We ask for this in the name of your Son, Jesus. Amen."

He was not surprised at the eyes looking at him as he opened his own and raised his head before finishing the prayer. In 1627, not only was being a Christian rare in Japan, but disclosing yourself as such could incite persecution and death. Men were to be loyal to their Shogun. Not an invisible, worse yet, *foreign* God.

Kai dispersed the men back to their stations.

"Every ship has a captain" was one of the last things Nobumasa said to Kai before leaving the Onsen. The phrase was enflamed in his mind as he watched it play out in real-time.

He looked around at each of his mates, doing their duty, fighting to keep the ship upright amid the storm, and knew Nobumasa spoke wisely. Rejecting the captain's authority puts individual lives at risk, but more importantly *for the Japanese, it destroys wa, putting the entire community at risk.*

Japan may be slow brewing, Kai thought, but eventually, they will know that it is not a coincidence that our culture is a perfect fit for our Creator's values. And when that happens, it will be a glorious awakening bringing extraordinary joy to Japan, giving true meaning to the unique national identity (kokutai) every Japanese knows deep in their heart.

A Rough Flight

Here's your cup of hot tea," the flight attendant said, placing the cup on Maria's tray.

"Thank you," Maria replied, looking at the cup of brown water. In two more hours, Maria would be landing in Shanghai. Her love for tea was one of the ingredients in Maria's fascination with China.

She lifted the string and swished the tea bag through the water to gauge how much more she should steep it. Finally, Maria raised the cup to her lips to take a sip.

"Lipton for now, but great tea is coming soon!" Maria whispered to herself as she placed the cup back on the tray in front of her.

Maria was a third-year math major at college in Frankfort, Germany. Just weeks ago, during her final exams, she decided she needed to spend the summer away. Away from her parents, her non-existent love life, and her pathetically pale mono-chromatic Germanic existence. At 21 years old, she was on her way to China, further away from home than she'd ever been without her over-involved parents.

Last semester she had barely kept up with school. Perhaps not depressed, but emotionally listless. She couldn't point to one thing that got her in this state of mind. It wasn't a breakup with a boyfriend, disliking her college, drug abuse, or any of the usual things that get off track. It was boredom. It was a stale passionless existence that made her realize *something* needed to change!

Her life had always been dependably ordered. From the moment she was born in Neubrandenburg, Germany, her existence was a pleasant and thoroughly saturated state of *boredom*.

It's hard to state that out load, though. People might judge Maria as having a bad attitude, snobby and ungrateful. This wasn't true of Maria. Deep in her core, she knew that adventure, passion, and purpose were possible. She had watched her friends seek it in all the familiar places, sex, drugs, educational achievement, and adrenaline sports. She had tried the last two; until last year, she'd been at the top of her class and was impressive in the skateboard park. But her observation of herself and all her friends was that they were coming up short on fulfillment.

China was going to change that. She had a good feeling about this new adventure. She was ready to take chances and find a vibrant palette to paint her *new* self-portrait. She spoke Mandarin quite well; she had started at three in preschool and continued through college. And her favorite teas were from China; Lapsung Suchung was top of the list, but she liked Jasmine and various oolong and green teas.

Her summer in China was poised to be adventurous (no set plans!), romantic (hopefully!), and self-fulfilling (*something* must be worth living for!). At a minimum, she would be out from underneath the ever-watchful eyes of her parents.

Maria took another sip of tea and opened a bag of trail mix her mom had packed. Suddenly, a commotion broke out in the front of the plane. What started as something banging on the floor led to shouts and screams as four men stood to their feet, each from a different position on the plane.

"Everyone, remain in your seats, do as we say, and no one will be hurt," one of the four men yelled loud enough for everyone on the plane to hear. "There are four of us with backpacks full of explosives and two others who will be taking control of flying the plane."

Everyone saw that the four men each had a backpack and a handgun. Two hijackers took someone from the plane hostage, wrapping an arm around each hostage's neck. Two other hijackers headed for the cockpit, demanding entrance or the hostages would be hurt. After a few minutes of intense arguing, the door to the cockpit opened. Two hijackers entered the cockpit and took control of the plane. The pilot and co-pilot were sent out to sit with the passengers.

Maria felt panic as her heart raced. Her palms became sweaty, and Maria's left leg began to shake involuntarily.

"Remain calm," the man sitting in the seat next to Maria whispered. "As long as we do as they say, these people benefit nothing from hurting us."

Many of the passengers on the plane began to cry and weep out loud.

"Be quiet," one of the hijackers shouted. He was standing just a few rows from Maria with his arm around one of the passenger's necks.

"Can I have your attention, please," a British accent said over the plane's intercom. "We now have complete control of the plane. We have made demands to the people on the ground in Shanghai. As long as our demands are met, no one on the plane will be harmed. Everyone must remain in their seat and quiet. We will silence you if you cannot do so on your own."

11

"Be quiet," the man sitting next to Maria said to the passengers sitting behind them. A couple of people sitting in rows close by were chatting with excitement about how they could overtake the hijackers. They discussed a plan for retaliating and getting the pilot back in the cockpit.

"Silence," one of the hijackers screamed as he walked up to the row where Maria was sitting. He pushed his hostage away and grabbed Maria by the arm, pulling her out of the seat.

"Do you have a problem following directions?" the man questioned her.

"No, sir," Maria replied. "It wasn't me."

"Who was it then?"

"I don't know," Maria answered. "It was coming from behind me."

The hijacker spun Maria around and held her by the back of her neck.

"Who back here has a problem following instructions?" the man demanded, tightening his grip on Maria's neck.

"Excuse me," the flight attendant said a little louder as she tapped Maria on the shoulder.

"Help!" Maria screamed as she jumped out of her seat on the plane.

Passengers turned and were straining to get a view of the distraction. Maria grabbed the seat in front of her, frantically looking around. No one had her by the back of the neck. There were no hijackers on the flight. It had all been a horrible nightmare.

"Are you alright?" the flight attendant asked.

"I'm sorry," Maria whispered, embarrassed by the commotion she had created. "It was just a bad dream. I'm so sorry."

Maria sat back in her seat, trying to hide her face from the other passengers wanting to look at her.

"We're getting ready to land," the flight attendant told her. "I need you to put your seatbelt on."

"Sure," Maria answered. "No problem."

Maria left the airport as quickly as she could, wanting to flee the embarrassing scene she'd created on the plane. She picked up a cab waiting outside the airport and headed for the apartment her parents had rented her for the summer.

Maria was surprised at the size of her new apartment. China was known for tiny living spaces. But her parents had arranged for a fully furnished one-bedroom apartment with a kitchen, living room, dining room, foyer, and a large bathroom.

She unpacked her luggage and then rummaged through the drawers and cabinets in the kitchen, getting an idea of what needed to be stocked. The clock hanging on the wall said it was just after 5:00 p.m. Shanghai time. Frankfurt was seven hours behind Shanghai. She quickly called to let her mom know that she'd arrived safely and everything was fine.

Maria glanced in the full mirror hanging on the inside of her bedroom door before hitting the streets of Shanghai for the first time. Her light brown hair lay straight just a few inches below her shoulders. She had round German cheekbones and fair skin. A size two dress, she took after her mom, thankfully; her dad was a large, stocky man.

Cute rather than exotically gorgeous was how people described her. She also had an air about her. One young man at college had told her, "You give people the impression you aren't available." Perhaps that was fitting for Maria. Men were immature, in her opinion. More interested in their own needs than hers.

As she looked at herself tonight, she thought about what was different. Somehow, in one plane ride, *she* was different. Maybe she felt more available. Not necessarily intimately, but just interested. Open. Willing to travel. Take chances. And *quite* ready to see what life would offer here in China.

She turned to see her profile and knew something certain: her pink sundress, tan flip-flops, and round eyes gave her away as a visitor to Asia. But she was okay with that. She grabbed her purse and keys and made her way into the streets of Shanghai for the first time. Freedom and adventure awaited.

Who Has More Power?

After two hours, the storm's wind was still strong, but the ferocious gusts had quelled.

It made things easier for the captain and his crew. Kai's mind had time to drift. He thought of how the Apostle Paul must have felt during the storm that caused the ship's wreck in the Book of Acts.

How ominous were the thunder and lightning during the storm? How strong would the wind gusts have been to cause the shipwreck? How would Paul have prayed amidst the storm?

In all of Kai's years at sea, being shipwrecked was perhaps the only sailing experience he had never had. He'd been lost at sea, had to sail for days without rations, dove into icy waters to rescue an overboard sailor, been rescued himself after being thrown overboard by a rogue wave, been pirated, witnessed a mutiny as a young lad, and had his ship blasted by cannon.

But Kai had never been involved in a shipwreck. He instinctively tapped the wooden captain's wheel for good luck as he said the words in his head.

"Whoops," Kai said out loud, "no more of that in my life. Heavenly Father, sorry. No more superstition. You are the God of all!"

Before spending time with his brother, he wasn't "against" the Christian faith. He didn't know enough or care to form an opinion. Kai was often at sea for weeks at a time. Aboard a ship, a man had plenty of time to let his thoughts and feelings meander, and most of those thoughts remained locked inside.

A year ago, Kai would not have noticed who prayed in a certain way or which good luck charm they felt would keep them safe. Sailing was inherently dangerous, so idols were common amongst sailors. Kai had his superstitions. For example, he had kept his beard long because he felt it had brought him luck when he could finally grow one. He idolized his dad and felt that his ancestor, the great samurai, was keeping him safe.

Sailors didn't typically question each other's idols nor challenge whose idol had more power. They were personal choices.

Nobumasa had challenged him, though. "Who do you think has more power to make a difference in your life? Your Creator God, your beard, or your ancestor?"

Logically, there was only one answer.

Kai checked his course settings and corrected the wheel slightly. The storm was not the worst Kai had seen, yet he felt unsettled. Maybe, he surmised, his nerves were a little tired after over a year on dry land. Or perhaps something else wasn't sitting right with his soul. Something felt wrong on the ship's deck.

"I need your feedback," Kai said to Enji as the second in command returned to the ship's wheel. "What are the men saying about my faith?"

Enji paused for a second before answering his captain. "I'll be honest," Enji replied. "It's causing a stir with one of them, and he is raising questions amongst the crew."

Kai's suspicions were accurate.

"What exactly is being said? Do you think my faith is costing me the crew's respect?"

Enji looked his friend square in the eyes. "Not with the men who are a regular part of the ship. They have spent too many years sailing under you for that to happen. While they might disagree with your beliefs, they won't allow their opinions to get in the way of their careers. They want to be a part of your crew long after this trip ends."

Kai could hear the hesitancy in his friend's voice. He knew a "but" was coming.

"You remember, Yìchén, the man catching a ride back home to China," Enji continued. "He is the one making the stir. He is questioning your leadership and masculinity. He has been persuasive. His questions and statements are causing some men on board to have their questions."

Kai stared off into the distance. "What do *you* think, though? Does my faith in Christ create questions for you?"

Enji chuckled out loud at his captain's question.

"Kai, nothing you do or don't believe could ever lead me to question your abilities to captain a ship," Enji replied. "Did hearing that you surrendered your life to something catch me off guard? Sure, it did. However, it's not affected my respect for you, our friendship, or your abilities as a trader and sailor. I'm on your side."

17

"I am concerned, though," Enji continued. "Yìchén is disturbed. Not only does he not believe in Jesus, it *really* bothers him that you do. So be careful, Kai. That's all I'm saying."

Kai lay on his bed staring at the ceiling alone in his captain's quarters. It was something in Enji's eyes when he warned Kai about Yìchén. Yìchén had been in Japan for a while, waiting on a ship headed for China. Japan's emperor had just issued some warnings that he would restrict the trade of foreign goods. At some unknown point in the future, no ships would be allowed anywhere but China and Korea; and all ports would be monitored closely.

Kai had gotten to know Yìchén in the two weeks leading up to Kai's voyage. Everything seemed good. Yìchén needed a ride to China, and the safest way to avoid attention from the authorities was to be hired as a deck hand. "Besides legalities, though," Yìchén had said, "it will be an honor to serve under a famous captain."

However, two days before deportation, Yìchén's prickly personality peaked when he found out Kai had become a Christian and had plans to bring his faith to China. Yìchén had decided he wouldn't jeopardize his ride, but he immediately started plotting against Kai. He aimed to teach Kai a lesson: there was no place for Jesus or the Bible in Asia, and certainly not in his home country of China.

A Handsome Cup of Tea

The neighborhood in Shanghai was flooded with both locals and tourists. Maria strolled the streets, noticing, two different groups of people. The locals moved through the streets on a mission, heads down, bobbing through the tourists as quickly as possible.

Contrastingly, the tourists had their heads up, taking in everything. Countless shops and vendors throughout the neighborhood sold souvenir items and essentials for the local community. The streets were electric with an energy that seemed big enough to light all of Germany.

With no plan, Maria chose a direction randomly and walked down several blocks. She noted where she could buy groceries, saw dozens of restaurants, and found two small coffee shops that advertised tea. She decided to sit and sample a cup before heading back to get groceries.

While she waited to be served, she delighted in the multicultural city — Asians, Europeans, South and North Americans. She even detected an Aussie accent. A busy hive of ethnically diverse bees making uniquely sweet honey. Maria smiled inwardly, ready for her first cup of Chinese tea *in China.*

"Good afternoon," a waiter stood at the end of Maria's table. "Are you interested in eating a meal, or would you prefer to see a menu of our local teas and coffee?"

The waiter wasn't at all what Maria was expecting. He was a young man around her age, attractive, tan, Caucasian and spoke perfect English.

"I'll just have a cup of tea this evening," Maria responded.

"Are you familiar with our choices, or do you need to see a tea menu?" the waiter asked.

"This is my first day in the city. I've never been here before," Maria informed him. "A few minutes to go over the menu would be great."

The young man handed Maria a laminated page with tea and coffee choices and promised to be back in a few minutes to take her order.

The waiter's good looks had caught her off guard. He had short blond hair with smiley green eyes. She guessed he was six feet tall and had two hundred pounds of gym-rat muscles.

"Do you have a personal favorite," she asked when he returned to take her order.

"Our fire blend has been my favorite since moving here," the waiter told her. "The tea leaves are grown at Oda Plantation, south of here, just outside Ningde. The leaves are seasoned by fire, giving them a unique flavor you cannot find anywhere else."

"Really? That sounds perfect. A Lapsung Souchong tea?" Maria asked.

"Well, generally, it would fit in that category, but the Oda Plantation feels their tea is sufficiently unique not to be labeled as such. You sound like you know tea well?"

"Oh, not really, but I am very interested." Maria's eyes sparkled. The conversation and the view were both piquing her interest. "Please tell me more."

The waiter saw the glimmer in her eyes and smiled. "Well," he continued, "the Oda Plantation never uses the lower leaves. Instead, they only use the choicest upper leaves of the plant. Which technically means it's not a Souchong. Also, they developed a unique cultivar of the Camellia Sinensis plant that is perfectly suited to the plantation's altitude and soil. Lastly, they cold-smoke their tea using a particular type of short rock pine found in their hills. It's fabulous, in my opinion."

Maria smiled. She started to respond, but the words weren't there. She was *too* happy. Tea and a handsome waiter who understood tea; it couldn't get any better than this. China was off to a good start!

Her slight hesitation made him doubt his monologue. "Sorry, perhaps that was too much information. Anyway, can I get you a cup?"

Maria responded, "Perfect. I would love a cup. What was your name again?"

"My name is Sebastian," the waiter told her.

"How long have you been here in Shanghai?" Maria asked.

"I moved here three years ago with my dad. I'll be honest, that's why I am your waiter. I usually help the customers who speak English to improve their experience here. The easier it is to order, the better the tea tastes."

He tilted his head, smiled, and left.

Maria smiled. His head tilt was adorable.

"Here you go," Sebastian said as he placed a cup of tea on the table in front of Maria. "I'm anxious for you to try a sip and tell me what you think."

Maria raised the brew to her nose, smelled the steam, and said, "Ooooh, I think I am going to like this. The nose is divine."

She then took a slow sip of the tea.

"Oh wow," she said, placing the cup back on the table. "This is fabulous!" She took another long sip as the waiter continued watching in the delight of Maria's approval. "I think this might be the best tea I have ever tasted. It's unique and complex, and the smoke is just right. I love its slight bitterness and the lovely floral finish."

"I know. It's out of this world, isn't it? This tea has been in our region since the 1600s. It's a local specialty that is largely undiscovered. The big commercial tea plantations own the worldwide markets, but the Oda plantation is special."

"And you said it's grown around here?" Maria asked.

"Yes, it's about a six-hour train ride to Ningde. The Oda Plantation is a little hamlet west of the Ningde, called Leiya. The hamlet is named after one of the former owners of the plantation. There is some cool history there from the 1600s, too. But today, the Oda Plantation still produces tea, has a campground, and is a place of respite for tea lovers. It's a place many people visit, especially Christians from Asia. Supposedly, it was one of the first places in China to have a Bible. But, regardless of your faith, and by the way, I'm not a Christian, it's a place you should visit."

"I might need to check this out," Maria told him. "Today is my first day in Shanghai," she continued. "How difficult is it to get familiar with the train system?"

"It can be tricky," Sebastian answered. "If you're up for it, I get off work early the day after tomorrow and have the following day off. We could head down right after I leave work, spend the night at the campground, and come back the following day. It's too long of a trip to just spend a few hours at the plantation."

Maria pierced her lips together and gave the waiter a devilish grin before picking up her cup of tea and taking another sip.

"Let me think about that while I finish this," she told him. "I try not to get in the habit of being gone overnight with a guy I have just met."

Sebastian laughed out loud at Maria's answer and the look on her face.

"I am a good guy, but I understand," he answered. "I will bring you back something to eat in a few minutes. Just a small gesture to show you can trust me. Then, I'll take care of the bill."

Maria nodded her head. "I could use something to eat. Thank you."

Maria ate the dish of noodles and beef and enjoyed a second cup of tea before leaving. As she ate, she felt her intuition leading her to agree to make the trip with her new friend for a night of camping at

Oda Plantation. Uncharacteristic for conservative Maria, she found her lips telling Sebastian, "Yes, I would like to go to the Oda Plantation with you."

She told herself that with the voyage still two days away, she had plenty of time to research the plantation and make sure her friends back home knew where she would be. In addition, Maria planned to revisit the coffee shop the next day while he was working, just to get to know him better before the trip.

Back at the apartment, Maria sat on the balcony and watched the sun go down. She closed her eyes and allowed the neighborhood sounds to penetrate her mind. The area was still busy, even with night falling. She could hear passing traffic below, and conversations as people tried to talk loud enough to be heard while coming and going. Maria listened to the family in the apartment next to her as they gathered for dinner. The night was filled with chaos, business, and pleasure, creating a beautiful sound of humanity living out loud.

With her eyes still closed, Maria slowly traced over the day. It didn't start smoothly. Traffic accidents caused delays getting to the Berlin airport, and she barely made the flight. Then, she embarrassed herself with a loud overreaction when the flight attendant woke her from a dream.

But it got better. Once she got to her beautiful apartment and made plans for an overnight getaway with a handsome, tea-loving man, she felt like a sprinter inspecting the track in Beijing—an explosive start, precise form, and strong finish would bring a gold medal. She felt *this* was going to be the best summer of her life.

Thinking of an explosive start, the nightmare on the plane could not have been more dramatic. Dreams were not typical for Maria; when she dreamt, they were, at worst, zany. But this one was scary.

She reflected further, letting her science and math-oriented mind search for a cause or meaning. Was it flying? Decidedly not, flying was fun for Maria. Was she nervous about getting to China? Honestly, she was a little worried about leaving home and being alone in a foreign country.

The nightmare on the plane had seemed real, and playing it back in her mind, it was like a movie. She could remember many details of the aircraft, the hijackers, and the other passengers on the plane. She shuddered involuntarily. Fear and embarrassment are a toxic and humiliating combination.

Maria willed herself out of the chair and resolved to have a peaceful night's sleep. It had been an exhausting day. She was ready for the first night of sleep in her new home away from home.

Maria changed into pajamas, brushed her teeth, and crawled into the queen-sized bed. She texted her mom to let her know the first day in Shanghai was over. She sent a few messages to friends through social media, then put her phone on the nightstand next to the bed.

The pillow felt good.

Something caught her eye on the table. Maria was in a room with a single small table in the middle. The room had no windows, and only one doorway opened into a long, dark hallway. She slowly turned around, looking at each wall. They were empty, a milk-white reflection of her listless life. Her attention then went back to the table. There was a photo album, a blank sheet of paper, and an ink pen.

Maria gently opened the photo album's cover and looked at the first page. It was a picture of her mom holding a newborn baby in a hospital. Maria had seen her baby picture a thousand times. The same image was framed on the desk in Maria's bedroom at home. Still, the picture was different in this photo album. She was not sure what was different but felt there might be a hidden message she had never noticed before.

Captivated, Maria sat down in the chair at the table, pulling the photo album closer.

Each page had a familiar photograph from her life. She knew these photos; they were in order from the day she was born. Birthday parties, her first bicycle, a trip to the beach, precious friends, and the three houses of her youth. These were all the important moments of her life, invoking happy memories.

Until the last two pages. Here she found a picture of herself sleeping on the plane to China. Maria inspected the expression on her face in the photo. She looked afraid and concerned; it was taken during her dream.

Maria turned the page.

She gasped. It was a picture of her sitting at the coffee shop laughing with Sebastian.

Who had taken these last two photographs?

Maria pulled the photo album closer to get a better view. She was able to recognize the look on the waiter's face. Who had taken the photo? How was it here? The picture was taken at the exact moment Maria agreed to go to the campground for the night.

Maria suddenly realized there was a handwritten note underneath the last image.

"This has been your life up to this point," the paper said. "You have had plenty of good in your life, but what have you accomplished that has made life better for someone else? This is the summer of change. Don't miss the wisdom and transformation that comes with the tea!"

Making Plans with The Devil

A few days later, Kai walked out of his captain's quarters onto the ship's deck. The skies were cloudless indigo and his disposition matched the sunny heavens. Kai knew he had slept longer than he'd planned by the sun's brightness and position in the sky.

"You're awake," Enji snickered as Kai approached the ship's wheel.

"How long did I oversleep?" Kai asked.

Enji laughed. "You got exactly as much sleep as you needed, captain. It's been smooth sailing the last three or four hours. We should hit land in around 10 or 11 hours at this pace," Enji said. "You needed rest. You were mentally drained when you finally called it a night. Knowing you, you probably didn't retire to your quarters and immediately fall asleep. I'm sure you had a lot going on between your ears."

Kai laughed. "You know me too well, my friend. I feel refreshed and at peace. Let me take over for a while. I'm sure you could use a break from the wheel."

"I won't argue with that," Enji responded. "I'm going to take a walk around the ship and see how everyone's feeling with our progress. Then, I'll let you know before I close my eyes for a nap."

28

Kai briefly peered through a telescope. It looked like a great day to hit the port and start his trip inland. Not only was the sea's surface smooth, but there wasn't a single ship on the horizon.

With the waters calm, Kai's mind wandered. Nobumasa had spent years creating the scrolls to teach others the Bible in a way the Asian could comprehend and fit into their worldview. He had taught Kai that Jesus' message of love toward everyone had to be delivered so that people could hear it. Nobumasa had said that if people heard 'foreign God,' we said it wrong. If people heard 'wrathful God,' we said it wrong. We said it wrong if people heard *anything* but who God said He is. "It's a big responsibility. We must say it the way Jesus and the Apostles said it."

"So for you," Nobumasa continued, "you can't say it right if you aren't living it right. *Read it, Believe it, Live it.* Said another way, Listen, Learn and Obey. You *must* live this way. And when you do," his brother told him, "That is where indescribable joy is found!"

Kai was known in the port cities and villages of China. Everyone who made their living trading goods knew him and that he was trustworthy. However, the further Kai went inland, the less valuable his reputation would be.

Kai had initially planned on talking with Yìchén about the possibility of introducing him to a few people who could help Kai find tea plantations in the low mountains west of Shanghai. Yìchén was a local, and it seemed likely he would have valuable connections. However, with so many questions concerning Yìchén's acceptance of Kai's Christian faith, Kai had second thoughts.

"Captain," Kai heard, redirecting his attention to his surroundings instead of his prayers. "Is there anything specific you want me to accomplish before we reach land?" Yìchén asked.

Kai had deliberately avoided any contact with Yìchén. Now, the two of them stood almost face-to-face. No one else was close enough to hear them. This was the perfect opportunity if Kai wanted to speak with Yìchén.

"Have you completed everything Enji asked you to do?" Kai questioned.

"Yes, sir," Yìchén responded. "Everything has been done that was assigned to me. I asked you because I'm grateful for the ride home and can provide more help if needed."

Kai was left with a question. Should he ask or not? If Kai were going to ask him for help, he wouldn't get a better opportunity.

"Do you live in Shanghai, or was it just the closest port to your home?" Kai questioned.

"Born and raised," Yìchén told him. "If I'm not working at sea or in another land, Shanghai is home. My house is just a few minutes from where we will dock the ship."

"What is the longest you have been away from home on one trip?" Kai was trying to buy a few minutes to decide how far to take the conversation. The more information he was willing to give would guide the rest of Kai's conversation. Plus, Kai was observing how friendly Yìchén would respond.

"These previous four months have been the longest I have been away from home in one trip," Yìchén told Kai. "Your emperor's threat of restrictions made it difficult to find a ship heading back home. That's why I was interested in being a part of this voyage as soon as I heard about it."

"Has sailing always been your primary source of income?" Kai needed to keep the conversation going as long as he could. How far could Yìchén be trusted? There was a chance that even if he had no interest in becoming a Christian, if the reward was suitable, maybe Yìchén could introduce Kai to someone who would like to be a part of the mission.

"I trade," Yìchén said. "As you know, that includes much more than sailing. I get goods to the port as far as 100 miles from Shanghai. I also move goods from the port to where they can fetch the best price. That isn't always close to the sea. If there's a profit, I want to be part of the deal in one way or the other."

"The plan has been for me to remain in China for a while after we port," Kai admitted, "possibly even traveling inland. I need to find some tea plants that will grow in the mountains back in Japan. It's a project my brother and I are working on together. There will be money involved with finding these plants."

Yìchén shifted his weight from one leg to the other as he stared into Kai's eyes. "Are you offering me more work, captain?" he asked.

Kai responded without hesitation. "Yes, the deal would be you guiding me inland to find the tea plants."

Kai stopped for a brief second to look for any sign of enthusiasm on Yìchén's face. Unable to identify what he was looking for, Kai picked up where he had left.

"Everyone else onboard the ship will be returning home under Enji's command. I don't want to tie up the ship in port while researching the tea plants; it could take weeks. Therefore, we plan to unload, restock, and then set sail for home."

Kai walked to the ship's railing and looked across the water. He wanted to give Yìchén a few moments to digest the offer. Kai hadn't been sure he wanted to extend the offer. But it was out there now.

Kai turned to Yìchén and couldn't hold back. He continued to talk, almost as if the words were forced out of him. Ideas were coming to his head.

"The more I think about it," Kai continued, "It will take more than two of us to bring the tea plants back to Shanghai."

Yìchén moved closer to Kai, leaning against the ship's rail himself. This was leading to the opportunity he wanted. Yìchén couldn't have planned this out any better himself.

Kai continued, "Once we arrive at port, how long would you need to put together a crew of three or four men who could leave on this trip? We would make sure there was an agreement on everyone's pay before leaving Shanghai. Of course, you would make a little more for putting everything together on short notice. Those details can stay between the two of us."

Kai eagerly waited for a response. He could tell that Yìchén was quickly processing everything in his mind. Not just anyone could find three or four people willing to leave home for weeks, maybe even months, on short notice.

"Captain, you know yourself, the first question out of any man will be about the wages," Yìchén responded. "What should I tell them?"

Kai took his time with an answer. He didn't want to sound desperate. At the same time, he needed to be firm with his answer. Kai didn't want to have to negotiate with each man individually. He wanted to give a price most would find interesting.

"Put together a team of three or four dependable men. I will pay them 175 percent of a day's wages at the dock, per day. Ensure the men know they should expect to be away from Shanghai for around 25-40 days. I will give you 225 percent of a day's wages at the dock."

Yìchén paced for a brief minute or two, stroking his beard in thought. He was in the same spot as Kai. Yìchén didn't want to sound too excited. He was willing to take any offer to have the captain to himself. Though, the more money up front, the better. Yìchén knew there would not be a long trip searching for tea leaves. Just a few hours is all the time Yìchén would need to teach Kai there was no place for Jesus Christ in Asia.

"Are you willing to give the men some of their pay before leaving on the trip? Remember, captain, while these men may have heard of your name, they don't know you. So, it might be easier to put a team together if they were given a portion of their pay up front."

Kai took a few steps in the other direction. He had to admit that Yìchén's request was fair.

Kai turned and faced Yìchén, "I will pay for ten days up front on the wages I mentioned earlier. Then, when we arrive back in Shanghai, I will pay the balance."

Yìchén showed no hesitation. He walked straight to Kai and bowed. "You have a deal, captain."

Yìchén pushed further to put his plan in motion. "Have you already arranged to stay in Shanghai for a day or two before we set off on our trip?"

Yìchén didn't wait for an answer. "My place isn't the biggest, but I can provide you with a comfortable place to sleep, good food, and all the rice wine you can drink for a day or two. So, we can relax and take it easy tonight. I'm sure a few friends might stop by for a drink or two, maybe even a potential man for the job. I can finish building the team tomorrow, and we could leave the next morning."

Kia hadn't had a drink of alcohol in over fourteen months. Alcohol had been a problem for Kai, on and off, throughout his adult life. His brother didn't drink and insisted that if Kai were going to stay with him, he had to be sober. God met him in sobriety and gave him the strength to stay sober. It was a freedom Kai had not expected, but now that the slave chain broke, he loved it.

Not knowing what to say, Kai responded, "I like that. As a matter of fact, why don't you consider your trip finished as soon as we dock. Just leave me directions to make it to your place."

"Are you sure the crew won't need help unloading cargo?" Yìchén asked.

"No, that's fine," Kai told him. "Hopefully, this was the first of many voyages we have together."

Kai hesitated. "You can do me one favor, though."

"Anything," Yìchén replied.

"I would appreciate it if you said nothing about rice wine to the other men on the ship. They all know that I said I no longer drink alcohol."

"No problem, captain; the way I look at it, the others don't even need to know you're staying with me." Yìchén winked. He liked knowing something Kai didn't want others to know. He had even more leverage now. His plan was coming together.

As Yìchén walked away, Kai remembered that something was bothering him before. Did he step into it or avoid it?

It's a Date!

Maria frantically sat up in her bed, gasping for breath. Not familiar with the surrounding, she jumped out of bed to her feet, forgetting where she was.

It finally sank in that she was in her bedroom, in her new apartment.

"It was just another dream," Maria spoke audibly. "What is going on?"

Maria headed to the kitchen to grab a bottle of water from the fridge. She unlocked the patio door and walked out onto the balcony. It was deep into the night, the sky was thick ink, the air smelled like a city, and the neighborhood below was still busy.

Maria's mind slowed as she looked out over the streets below. Had someone taken pictures of her, or were those only details of her dream? The last part of the letter stuck in her head.

"This is the summer of change. Don't miss the wisdom and transformation that comes with the tea!"

Sebastian had said the tea was special, but how could tea be a source of wisdom and transformation?

Maria went back into the bedroom to grab her phone. It was after 2:00 a.m. Shanghai time. Her alarm clock was set for 6:00.

Maria laid back down, hoping to sleep a little longer before it was time to wake up. Instead, she tossed and turned, replaying both of her dreams since leaving Frankfurt. Were the two somehow connected? Maria could count on one hand how many dreams she'd had over the last twelve months. Now, two dreams in 24 hours seemed ominous to her.

The morning was spent making a second trip for groceries and familiarizing herself with the neighborhood. Once Maria was settled back into the apartment, she got out her laptop and looked up the Oda Plantation. There was a campground, tours of the plantation, and the place was well known with hundreds of four- and five-star reviews. Everything Sebastian had told her appeared to be legit.

Maria returned for a late lunch to the coffee shop where Sebastian worked. Within a few minutes of sitting at an empty table, her favorite Shanghai waiter showed up to take her order.

"Are you ready for tomorrow?" Sebastian asked as he approached Maria's table.

"Yes," she answered. "Well, sort of. I checked out the website this morning. It looks like an exciting place to visit. But where should I buy a tent and sleeping bag?"

"No worries," Sebastian answered. "I have an extra sleeping bag you can borrow. And we will rent two tents at the campground. Plus, Ningde has a great camping store. We will take the train down to Ningde, pop into the store for some things and then take a bus ride to the plantation. You are going to love it. Do you want something to eat or just another cup of tea?"

"I'm starving," she answered. "I'm ready to eat. How about some shrimp fried rice if you have it?"

"Coming right up," Sebastian replied.

"And some egg rolls?" Maria said after he turned.

While she ate her lunch, Maria watched how Sebastian interacted with the other customers. He seemed kind and attentive. She didn't have a "good enough" or "not good enough" column for people. But, she was about to spend two days with a man she had just met—camping in a small tent next to his! She was up for an adventure, *maybe* even a slow brewing romance, but not at the cost of her conservative values. Maria was cautious with men.

Sebastian finally came and sat in the chair across from her as Maria finished the last couple bites of her meal.

"How long since you've been to the plantation?" Maria asked.

"I was there earlier this spring with a few friends. We make the trip now and then to get away for a few days. It's nice to escape the busy noise of Shanghai. Plus, there is something special there. I can't put words to it. You'll see."

"And," he added, "I'm looking forward to cooking for you over an open fire instead of taking your order and giving it to someone else."

"Wow. How gentlemanly of you. I like that." She smiled warmly.

Sebastian smiled too but then looked away shyly as if he was suddenly embarrassed by her reaction to him. This was an excellent sign for Maria. Shy worked, given that they were about to sleep just a few feet from each other, separated by two thin sheets of ripstop nylon.

Maria asked, "When and where are we meeting tomorrow?"

"That's up to you," Sebastian answered. "You can either meet me here, and we'll head to the train station together, or we can meet at the station. What works best for you?"

"What time should I meet you here? I'd rather have you do all the navigating."

"Meet me here at 10:00 tomorrow morning," he said. "I'll get online this evening, buy our train tickets, and make reservations at the campground."

"Sounds great, Sebastian. Thank you."

"Here's my number," he said while jotting the digits on the back of Maria's receipt. "Call me if anything comes up. If not, I'll see you tomorrow morning at ten."

"It's a date," Maria said.

Maria winced. The words were out of her mouth before she could stop them. It was *not* a date!

Then to make it more awkward, she laughed nervously.

Sebastian flushed, turned away quickly, and answered, "I'm looking forward to it." He hurried off to his duties.

Maria sat in a chair on the balcony of her apartment with her laptop. She scrolled social media and connected with some friends in Germany.

It was now just after 4:00 p.m. Shanghai time. Too late for a nap and far too early to go to bed. Still, Maria felt exhausted. She had been up early, woken from her dream.

She turned on the television for the first time since arriving in Shanghai and propped herself up with pillows on the couch. Maria flipped through the different channels for a few minutes, but nothing seemed to catch her attention. It didn't take long for her to drift off to sleep.

Maria sat on her knees behind a table about a foot from the floor. She watched as a middle-aged man took a pot of hot water from over the wood stove in what looked like a small, one-room shack. He brought the pot and two cups to the table where Maria was sitting.

She watched as the man's hands seemed to glide through the air in a specific rhythm. He put a spoonful of ground tea into each cup and filled them almost full with the water. Then, with specifically calculated movements, the man whipped the tea into a light froth, and placed the whisk upright on a holder in the middle of the table. He gestured for Maria to sip, watching for her approval without saying a word.

Maria recognized the drink as the fire-dried tea she had for the first time at the coffee shop where Sebastian worked. As good as that tea was, this cup was even better. It tasted fresh. The aroma was bright and clean as if the tearoom was suddenly a garden of tea plants.

She glanced around the small room, almost expecting to see a few potted tea plants sitting in the room. But all Maria could see was the small table, a few cushions on the floor, and a countertop with cups and small glass containers with tea grounds.

Each wall had an Asian scroll hanging on it, with another from the middle of the ceiling. A book was sitting on the edge of the table, with a notepad and a pen.

"Are you ready to start today's lesson?" the man finally asked.

Maria opened her eyes and sat up on the couch.

"What is going on inside my head?" she thought.

Maria stood up and went to the kitchen for a water bottle. She opened the door to the balcony, and the sounds of the busy neighborhood rushed in. She lifted her head and peered at the sky; a city haze distorted the sunlight.

It was time to get some advice. Maria pressed the button on her phone to call her mom.

She described each of the dreams to her mom, providing all the details. She included the distinct flavor of the tea in the latest dream. Maria shared the wisdom and transformation she was supposed to experience from the tea.

Maria's mom listened attentively.

"Maria, we share the same genes and we both can over-analyze things. It might make you feel better to do some journaling about the dreams. Date them and include as much detail as you have described to me. Chronicle them, and then look to see if the dreams are connected."

"But then," her mother continued, "enjoy the next couple of days at the campground. I know you. You have good judgment and good moral boundaries. Stay strong in those but take this time to focus on a friendship with Sebastian and see if you can set aside the dreams."

Maria felt much better after talking with her mom. She spent about an hour writing the entries in her computer journal. After replaying everything in her mind and reading through what she had written, Maria could not put any connection together other than the tea. The specific taste of the tea was authentic like it was supposed to get her attention. Maria closed the laptop and decided to take an evening walk through the neighborhood.

This walk was different from the others. She ventured out well past four blocks from her apartment. Also, Maria purposely engaged with other people in the busy streets. She asked the locals how their day had been and asked tourists and visitors about their origins. She found it refreshing to interact with other people, in a language she loved, in a country she felt she was coming to love.

On a bridge overlooking a small stream, Maria rested on a bench to enjoy the sunset. Soon, a man in an orange monk robe sat on the same bench. Without a word, he sat down and stared out at the sunset.

Still feeling talkative, she asked the monk, "Excuse me, sir, can I ask you a question? Do dreams mean something to you in your religion?"

He continued staring at the river spilling into the orange setting sun. He said a few short words with a breathless whisper, "The Tao is moving. Follow it."

He got up and slowly walked away without another word. Maria tried to ask him another question, but to no avail. He flipped his hood up as a sign of disengagement. He had said all he was going to say.

No Room For Foreign Gods

Kai had just finished his dinner when there was a knock at Yìchén's door. He'd been at Yìchén's house for a short while after finishing with the ship.

At Kai's command, Yìchén had left the ship as soon as it docked. In the three hours before Kai arrived, Yìchén was able to find two accomplices to help him end Kai's mission. Yìchén was going to make an example of what happens when someone brings a western god into his land.

He planned to punish, rob, and kill Kai before leaving him to be found at Shanghai's seaport. He didn't need to find four or five men to make a long trip searching for tea plants; Yìchén only needed to find a friend or two who would help him destroy Kai that night. A little alcohol was all he needed to take Kai by surprise.

The knock at the door let Yìchén know the fun was about to begin.

Kai was impressed with the physical build and stature of the two men Yìchén brought into the house. Of course, looks alone didn't always mean a strong work ethic and dedication, but Kai was impressed with what he saw.

"Kai, I would like to introduce you to Zǐmò (Zee-mo) and Hàoyǔ (How)."

Yìchén led his two friends toward the reclining area. As soon as Kai stood to introduce himself properly, both Zǐmò and Hàoyǔ bowed to greet their new acquaintance.

"We are honored to meet you, Mr. Kai," Zǐmò said. "Your reputation precedes you. My friend and I are honored to serve such a reputable trader and sea captain."

Kai bowed in response. "I assume Yìchén has given you the employment details and what the mission is?" he asked.

"Yes," Zǐmò replied, "the numbers are more than acceptable, and we appreciate the opportunity. I have two other men who couldn't make the trip tonight but will be here by midday tomorrow."

Yìchén interrupted the conversation. "Captain, we have just finished a trying voyage. Let us relax, enjoy the night with lots of wine, and make final arrangements tomorrow. Everyone knows the details of the work you've made available and have agreed to the numbers. We can discuss work and the details of our departure tomorrow. Let's enjoy the night, drink, and get merry. Let's sit outside by the fire, shall we?"

"Sounds great to me," Kai replied. Kai was ready to relax after his first voyage back at sea. He hadn't anticipated how exhausted his body was.

Yìchén seemed a little eager to get drunk, which raised a warning flag for Kai. Kai wasn't planning on drinking anyway, but now he was on full alert. Kai's rice wine would discretely make it to the ground.

The next couple hours were spent with the men drinking and sharing stories of life at sea. They traded tales of women, wealth, and heroic battles. The stories became more and more unbelievable as more alcohol was consumed — but they all laughed heartily. An observer might have thought the four men had been friends for decades.

Hàoyǔ had been the quietest through the night. At just 34 years old, he was the youngest and most robust in the group. He was massive, all muscle, with arms the size of thighs. He spent the least time divulging stories about his past.

Finally, Hàoyǔ asked a question that brought the group to complete silence.

"Mr. Kai, what exactly needs to happen for us to consider the trip we are about to take a success?"

Kai liked the question; it showed a desire to take responsibility for the trip's success. He looked down at the table in front of him. He was thoughtfully considering the question and how much to share. Kai finally broke his silence, feeling compelled to share the broader mission.

He slowly scanned each of the men at the table, one by one. Kai started, "The tea plants are important to my trip here in China. I need to find a species of tea that will grow and flourish in the mountainous regions of northern Japan. The tea is key to my family providing for ourselves and creating the financial security we need to keep our mission afloat."

Kai took a few brief seconds to breathe and look at each of the men again before continuing.

"But along with finding the tea plants to take home, I am on one of the most dangerous missions of my career. My brother and I believe that part of the reason I was created is to share the Gospel of Jesus

Christ throughout Asia, leading as many people as possible to surrender their lives to God."

Yìchén stood up and went around the room, filling the cups with wine. "Keep going, captain," he said. "You have my full attention. I just want to ensure everyone has enough to drink so you don't have to be interrupted."

"Thank you, my friend," Kai responded to what he perceived as a courtesy.

"This is a task I will never be able to complete on my own. I need to find a few other people ready to surrender their lives to Jesus and learn His teachings found in the Christian Scriptures known as the Bible. These aren't teachings Christians simply read. They are a way of living far greater than anything I have ever experienced. I wouldn't trade the relationship I now have with Jesus Christ for all of the wealth and fame in the world. Today, my life is far greater than anything I have ever experienced or imagined, and it's all because of my faith in Jesus Christ."

"Wait a second. I don't understand," Hàoyǔ questioned. "How can you say you have a relationship with Jesus Christ? Has He appeared to you in a dream? If you cannot see Him, how can you say that you have a relationship with Him?"

"Those are legitimate questions," Kai answered. "with logical answers. But, I can't provide the answers in a single conversation, especially with a mind clouded by alcohol. Perhaps we can discuss this more during our journey?"

Kai glanced at the other two men as they listened. "Also, it will be a great help if I have the scrolls and the Scriptures opened in front of me during the discussion, so I can explain how the Bible relates to your life."

The room went silent. Kai was able to catch both Hàoyǔ and Zǐmò looking at Yìchén as if they were waiting for approval. Kai could feel Yìchén's gaze upon him, but he quickly diverted his attention elsewhere when Kai turned to look at him.

"You have given us a lot to think about," Yìchén said, breaking the silence. "Perhaps you can teach us more when we start our journey and allow us to make our own conclusion on this relationship you speak of?"

Yìchén's mind considered options as he glanced across the table at his two friends.

Kai stood up from the table and walked to the nearby woods to relieve himself.

As soon as he was out of sight, Yìchén whispered to his two partners. "You see. As great of a sailor and trader he may have been at one time, this man has had his head filled with Christian nonsense. He believes this Jesus of the Bible is the only way of experiencing happiness and fame in this life."

Yìchén was building in anger. "We can't allow him to go through with this. Kai's name and reputation alone will cause many people to listen to what he says. Kai has to be stopped tonight!"

"What's the plan?" Hàoyǔ interrupted Yìchén. "Do you want to beat him and rob him? Or do you plan on killing him? I'm just as against stopping the spread of this religion as you are. But I am not in favor of killing a man. I want to ensure we are all on the same page."

Yìchén paused before answering the question. He didn't want to spook his friends into backing out if they knew murder was in the plan. "I want to beat him to a pulp, and I want him to know exactly why we're doing it. I don't want Kai to be able to walk. I want him to ache in pain every time he breathes. Let Kai see just how much Jesus can save him. We will keep his belongings and leave him at the port when we finish. I want to beat the belief out of him."

Kai returned to the fire and took his place at the table. He couldn't help but notice the way both Hàoyǔ and Zǐmò were staring at Yìchén. It was as if they were waiting on him to tell a story or ask a question. Finally, Yìchén stood up and excused himself from the table. He told the others it was his turn to use the woods. As he began to turn around to exit the room, Kai thought he saw Yìchén wink at the others.

Hàoyǔ started asking questions again. "What happened to lead you to find this relationship with Jesus," he asked.

Kai cleared his throat. "I spent the last 14 months with my brother, Nobumasa. He has studied the Bible for his entire adult life. He is the one who wrote out the tea room scrolls I will be teaching and spreading throughout Asia."

"Are these scrolls with you here?" Hàoyǔ asked.

"Yes," Kai replied. "I have them in the other room with the few belongings I have with me. I hope that maybe you will be interested in reading them in the coming days."

As soon as the words came out of Kai's mouth, he felt a fierce blow across the back of his shoulders, knocking him flat against the table. Debilitating pain shot down his spine and into his lower back.

Laying on his chest across the table, Kai turned his head just in time to see Yìchén raising a piece of wood above his head to deal another blow. Yìchén screamed as he swung the piece of wood in a downward motion, aiming for Kai's head.

Kai rolled across the table just in time to escape the fierce attack. Unfortunately, he wasn't ready for Zǐmò's elbow to come crashing into his jaw. Kai's face throbbed with pain as he quickly wrapped both arms around his head for protection. As soon as Kai's arms were raised, Yìchén drove the end of the branch into the center of Kai's stomach, causing him to jerk his knees up to his chin in agony.

Yìchén stood on the table and got down on his hands and knees next to where Kai was curled up in a ball. He wrapped his hand around Kai's neck, slamming the back of his head into the table.

"Did you think I would let you bring your talk of Jesus and Christian beliefs into my homeland?" Yìchén screamed. "You fool. There's no room for your foreign faith in Asia. *You* are not welcome here."

Yìchén lowered his voice to a hoarse demonic whisper, "I am going to kill you," he said calmly.

Yìchén stood back up on the table, straddling Kai's body. He drove the branch in the middle of Kai's stomach, slowly twisting it as if the pressure would guide the wood even deeper.

"The great ship captain and trader, Kai Oda, *thinks* he will come to my homeland and lead my countrymen astray with beliefs in a false god and religion," Yìchén screamed. "Not on my watch," he continued. "Over my dead body; yet you, my friend, are the one who will encounter death tonight."

To the one attacked by surprise, everything happens quickly. The first blow stuns and shocks the mind. The next one confirms that danger is indeed real.

One minute, Yìchén had left the fire. The next minute, Kai was being beaten with a piece of wood. Kai knew from his Bible studies that Jesus warned Christians may be persecuted. Persecution is what Kai's family feared. This is why Nobumasa had to grow up in a distant land in solitude. The beating Kai was going through was what his mother wanted to keep from her sons.

Kai was gasping for breath. The blow to his stomach had knocked the wind out of him. His shoulders ached with pain. Kai couldn't feel his face. Then, suddenly, out of nowhere, he experienced a great sense of peace and calm. His mind flashed with forgiveness for Yìchén, thankfulness to Jesus, and confidence that all would end well.

Kai closed his eyes and began to pray.

"Save me, Heavenly Father. Get me out of the mess I have created for myself. If it is your will for me to spread the Gospel message throughout this land, save me from the destruction I face."

Before he could finish his prayer, Hàoyǔ jumped up onto the table. In just a split second, he wrenched the log from Yìchén and blasted him across the face with it. The blow's force knocked Yìchén off the table, sending him tumbling onto the ground. Hàoyǔ sprang from the table onto the floor, slamming the piece of wood into Yìchén's back.

Stomping his boot on Yichen's head, Hàoyǔ quickly spun around, pointing the branch at Zǐmò.

"You have two seconds to make a choice," Hàoyǔ said. "You either stand there and watch us leave, or risk your life trying to stop us."

51

Zǐmò raised his hands to indicate he had no interest in being involved. He turned and hurried down the street.

Yìchén tried to climb back to his feet. He made it to his hands and knees before Hàoyǔ stepped into a half turn, kicking as hard as he could into Yìchén's stomach. Yìchén's body lifted off the ground, flipped over, and fell flat on his back. Hàoyǔ swung the branch, driving it into Yìchén's kneecap.

He then pinned Yìchén's neck to the ground while standing over him.

"You have the same decision to make," Hàoyǔ whispered just loud enough to be heard. "You either stay on the ground until you know we are gone, or you will lose your life tonight. What do you choose?"

Yìchén lay pinned to the ground, unable to feel his left leg. He didn't know if it was broken, but he knew his knee was dislocated.

"You are making a huge mistake," Yìchén hissed. "I will find you."

As soon as the words left his mouth, Hàoyǔ swung the piece of wood again with everything he had, this time making contact with the side of Yìchén's knee.

"What is your choice," he said again as Yìchén screamed in pain.

"Get out of here," Yìchén winced. "And don't ever stop running because I will find you."

Hàoyǔ turned his attention towards Kai, who was now sitting up on the table. "Are you able to walk?" Hàoyǔ asked.

Kai gave him a nod that he was good to go.

"Get your belongings," Hàoyǔ said.

Kai returned with his seabag strapped across his back. "I'm ready," he told his new friend.

Hàoyǔ gave Yìchén one last blasting in the other knee. There was a loud pop of wood smacking bone as Yìchén screamed. There was no question, this knee was knocked out of place. Yìchén rolled over onto his side, grabbing the dislocated knee.

Hàoyǔ and Kai exited the yard and made their way south through the roads of Shanghai.

"The quicker you can walk, the better," Hàoyǔ said to Kai. "We have to get out of town as fast as possible. Yìchén won't be going anywhere soon, but he has men that will be on the trail when they learn you are a Christian here to introduce others to Jesus. If we keep a quick pace, we can be in Hangzhou in less than a day. If you have the money, we can buy horses either on the way or when we get there. We have to move quickly and quietly."

In dead silence, the two men made their way several miles out of Shanghai. Not a word was spoken. They communicated with slight nods and hand gestures.

The fastest route from Shanghai to Hangzhou was a well-worn trail heading southwest. Hàoyǔ guessed that within an hour or two, if not sooner, Yìchén would have his thugs out searching for the men.

Kai couldn't walk fast, and Yìchén's men would have something Kai and Hàoyǔ didn't: horses. So, Hàoyǔ decided it was best to stay close enough to the trail that they could find it but far enough away that they were out of sight. As a result, if Yìchén's men caught up, they would not be found.

As severe of a beating Kai had taken before the getaway, Hàoyǔ was surprised at how well he could still move. Kai was eleven years older and injured, but he could keep up a good pace. Decades at sea had beaten him much worse than a man with a branch could do in a few minutes.

Once Kai felt they were far enough from Shanghai and out of ear's range from anyone on the nearby trail, Kai finally broke the silence between them.

"How can I repay you?" he quietly whispered.

Hàoyǔ continued in silence for several steps before responding. "I was sincere with my questions before what happened tonight," he replied. "My father was a Christian. His faith led to his public execution in Shanghai when I was a child."

The men continued in silence for several seconds before Hàoyǔ continued. "I can still remember watching my father pray as a child. My sister and I regularly asked our dad about his morning routine in his "quiet" place. He would always tell us that we didn't need to know until we were older. I don't think this was because he didn't want us to know Jesus. He knew that we were kids. One accidental slip of the tongue and our entire family would have been killed instead of just him."

Hàoyǔ tilted his head back and gazed up at the stars as they walked for a few seconds.

"I want to experience this relationship with Jesus you mentioned at the house. I want whatever you and my father are willing to risk your lives for. Some missionaries came through Shanghai during my adult life. I was interested in what they had to offer. But, I was too afraid to pursue where my heart was being led."

"To be completely honest," Hàoyǔ continued, "my courage tonight was not my own. I can only say that I saw a chance to have what cost my father his life, and at that second, I was willing to fight for it. It's as if I could hear my father telling me, 'It is now or never. If you want to experience blessings beyond anything you have ever imagined, you must do something now. This man will show you the way.'

Hàoyǔ stopped walking and turned to look Kai square in the eyes. Then, as silently as he could, Hàoyǔ whispered, "If you want to repay me for tonight, teach me to find what my father had."

He turned and continued walking as if nothing had been said.

Kai remained quiet for several more steps. Kai believed he was honest and had a heartfelt desire to be introduced to Jesus.

He acknowledged he would teach Hàoyǔ.

But Kai realized they needed a plan. As a captain at sea, he always had a plan.

"We need a plan. What happens after we buy horses in Hangzhou?" Kai quietly asked.

"Well, how did you and Yìchén cross paths?" Hàoyǔ questioned.

"The voyage to Shanghai was my first trip at sea in over 14 months. The emperor threatened to ban most trading out of the country, so there weren't many ships heading to or from China. We began planning our trip about three weeks before the journey began. Yìchén had been stranded in Japan for months, waiting for a ride home. He had heard about our trip around the port and introduced himself to me. He explained his stranded condition and his need for a way back to Shanghai, so I made room for him on the roster."

Hàoyǔ briefly snickered to himself. "That's Yìchén for you," he remarked. "Able to look anyone in the eyes and tell whatever lie it takes to get what he needs."

"What do you mean?" Kai asked.

"Yìchén was never stranded in Japan. He had to flee Shanghai about a year and a half ago for killing two of the emperor's soldiers. They turned Shanghai upside down, looking for him. There were all kinds of rumors. Some believed Yìchén had fled to Vietnam or even Korea. A few rumors started floating around that he had taken to the life of a sailor. After the emperor spent six months searching far and wide, he finally announced that his men had found Yìchén and killed him. Once he felt the emperor had given up the search, Yìchén decided it was safe to return home. Today was his first day back after being away for a very long time."

"How does this help us formulate a plan?"

"My point is," Hàoyǔ explained, "Yìchén will go to any lengths necessary for revenge. He isn't opposed to murder, even if that means killing the emperor's men. He is going to have people looking for us until we are found. He mentioned your Christian faith when he told us his plans to attack you. I don't have to tell you how dangerous that is. On top of that, he let us know you were carrying a lot of money. Yìchén only wanted you dead because of your faith. He doesn't need your wealth. He will promise that and more to whoever brings him our heads. We are not safe, Kai. There will be many

56

people looking for us for a long time. They will go to any lengths for the reward offered."

Kai took a few minutes, allowing the information to sink in. His original plans were to meet Enji and the ship back in Shanghai in 40 days. Unfortunately, Kai would have to place himself just minutes away from where the attack had happened to return home as planned. He wouldn't have the opportunity to inform Enji of any changes. Kai's second in command would wait around Shanghai's port for a few days. After that, they would set sail to return home to Japan.

Kai's thoughts drifted to a lesson in the tea room with his brother Nobumasa. Jesus had taught His followers to keep their attention on today. There was no need to fear or panic over tomorrow. Today would have enough troubles of its own. If Kai and Hàoyǔ were unable to reach Hangzhou to buy horses, there was no need to worry about making it back to the port in Shanghai 40 days from now.

Hàoyǔ quietly continued, breaking Kai's focus.

"I've never been there before, but there's a small tea plantation outside Ningde. We will be able to make it there in just a few days on horseback. The woman who owns the plantation is known for hiding away people on the run. She allows them to work as a laborer on her plantation for room and board. She is well respected. If we can make it there, we will be able to buy enough time to develop further plans. Besides, there is a small port in Ningde, which gives us more options. We may even be able to export your tea plants from there. Therefore, I believe we should try to make it to that plantation as quickly as we can."

Kai said, "I like that plan. Let's stop for just one second. I know you won't understand just yet, but I will begin teaching you when the

57

time is right. For now, I need you to believe I love the same Jesus Christ your father did."

Hàoyǔ looked at Kai's eyes as if he could find Kai's faith and clone it for himself. Instead, he realized he needed to believe Kai. "I have faith," he said. "I believe that you know my father's Jesus."

Kai closed his eyes and placed his hands on Hàoyǔ shoulders. "Yes, I do. I know your Father's Jesus. I can't wait until we have more time to make a better introduction."

Kai deeply inhaled and then breathed the air out slowly.

"Heavenly Father, thank you for the opportunity you have blessed me with to meet Hàoyǔ. Thank you for the courage he found to save me from the evil planned against me. Use me to guide him closer to Your Son, Jesus. If it is your will, Father, use this man of courage to help us get to safety and share the Gospel message. Wrap your hands around us, Father, and protect us from the evil set out against us. Lord, use us for your glory. We love you and ask for this in the name of your Son, Jesus. Amen."

Tea That is Too Hot to Handle

Maria filled the small pot with water from the faucet and then placed it on top of the wood stove. She walked to one of the windows to look outside while the water heated. Outside was a well-used fire ring with a stump for seating. Maria went outside to get a better look.

She sat down on the stump next to the fire pit. She thought about the phone conversation she'd had earlier. Her mom told her to enjoy the peace and serenity of being outdoors. Maria closed her eyes and allowed her mind to relax. Immersed in the surroundings, her face softened as the tension drained.

Her concentration was broken by the sound of a familiar voice.

"There you are," said the older man who had made her tea in the previous dream. "Your water was finished, so I made you a cup of tea. I see you have found my ancestor's fire pit. This is where Kai would sit to pray and meditate on the lessons he would teach, the same lessons you are learning now."

The older man stepped closer to Maria, handing her the cup of tea he'd made. Maria took the cup, but it was too hot for her to handle. She instinctively pulled her hands back, dropping the teacup on the ground.

"I'm so sorry," Maria said as she jumped to her feet.

"That's okay," the older man said. "Don't worry. This is the lesson you have been pondering in your mind since the last time we spoke."

"What do you mean?" Maria asked.

"You came to my family's campground looking for tea," the man said as he bent down and reached for the spilled cup.

He picked up the cup. But by the time he stood up, the cup was gone, and he was holding something in his fist. He took Maria's hand, straightened her fingers out flat, and then placed a small gold pendant in her hand.

"This represents the wisdom and transformation you were warned not to miss."

Maria inspected the pendant closely, and then woke up. It was another dream.

She put her feet on the floor while she sat on the edge of her bed. She looked at her empty hand; she clenched and unclenched it as if to make the pendant come back magically.

Her dreams were speaking to her, enticing her with bits of information that seemed related but incomplete. While she had no information on the origin of the pendant, Maria knew that the man had told her it represented the wisdom and transformation she wasn't supposed to miss while searching for tea.

Still, in her latest dream, the older man revealed that the shack belonged to his family. Where and what was this place, and why was his family so relevant? The man had mentioned someone named Kai teaching lessons and that Maria was learning, too. How was Kai important, and what lessons was Maria preparing to take?

A couple hours later Maria was at the café, ready to leave for the tea plantation. "You're about 30 minutes early," Sebastian said to Maria as he approached the table. Her small backpack was propped against a leg of the table.

"That was the plan," Maria replied with a laugh. "I was hoping I would have time to grab a bite to eat before we left?"

"That works out great," he answered. "Tell me your pleasure, and I'll put the order in now."

Sebastian returned with Maria's rice rolls about 10 minutes later. "I made sure they're spicy," he told her.

"Perfect," Maria said. "How was work this morning?" she questioned.

"Things have been slow for the most part. I'll be cleaned up and ready to go in about 20 minutes. Do you have everything you need for the trip?"

"Yes, I am ready!"

"Awesome, I'll get things wrapped up, and then we have plenty of time to get a cab to the train station. I'll see you in a few minutes."

Sebastian returned wearing a different outfit and a backpack. It was the first time she had seen him wearing anything other than his work uniform. Sebastian instantly transformed from a cute waiter into a handsome man. His tan was even more attractive in the khaki cargo shorts and light green, button-up, short-sleeved shirt.

"I'm all set," Sebastian informed her. "Are we ready to go?" he asked as he sat at the table across from Maria.

Suddenly, Maria's mind laser focused. The top button on Sebastian's shirt was unbuttoned.

"Where did you get that?" Maria asked, pointing at the necklace Sebastian was wearing. It was a thin leather strand with a dull metal pendant.

Maria reached up and took the piece of metal hanging from his neck in her hand. It was the pendant from her dream, the wisdom and transformation she was supposed to pursue.

"You like that?"

Maria stood to her feet. "I'm serious, Sebastian," she said. "Where did you get that?"

"It's from the plantation gift shop at the campground," he answered. "That is the only place where you can get them. The pendant is somehow related to the Oda family that owns the plantation. I can't remember the whole story, but I always wear it at the plantation so they know I have been there before."

Sebastian also stood up, causing the pendant to rise out of Maria's hand. "It's just a souvenir necklace. We can get you one if you want when we get to the plantation. Is everything alright?"

"Yeah, I just thought it was something... er... Well. Yes. Let's get going."

When they got settled on the train, Maria asked, "You had said that the plantation has a cool history. I know you don't remember the full story behind the pendant, but can you tell me what you know?"

"Sure. So, Leiya was the owner of the plantation. I think this was the 1600s. One day a son of the famous samurai Oda Nobunaga, can't remember the son's name, came to the plantation to buy tea plants to take back to the mountains in Japan. He was a Christian and brought with him a way of studying the Bible in a tearoom. This was a cool fit because, of course, this was a tea plantation. The plantation has his name, yet the town is named after her. I don't know why because she is the one who owned the plantation. We can ask about that, but anyway, back to Leiya; you will like her. She was a strong independent woman in an era and culture when that was not accepted. Among Asian women today, she is like a heroine. You'll probably want to get a book there—she is like a saint or something. That's about all I remember."

"What about the pendent, though?"

"Oh yeah," Sebastian said, reaching for his pendant and turning it over in his hand. "I'm pretty sketchy on this. It is somehow interesting to Christians. A connection to Japan, I think? I'm sorry. We will have to ask when we get there. I remember it being cool when they told me, but now I can't remember."

The six-hour train ride couldn't get over fast enough. It's not that Maria didn't enjoy the time talking with Sebastian and getting to know him better. She just kept finding her mind drifting back to the pendant.

Within an hour of being on the train, Maria asked Sebastian if he would take it off so she could get a better look at it. The coloring was different than her dream. The gift-shop souvenir was a dull-gold metal color, but the one from her dream was a different shade of gold.

Other than that, the necklace she was holding looked the same. There was a symbol on one side of the pendant. On the other side was a cross and writing along the circular edge. Maria couldn't wait to get to the plantation and learn its meaning.

Ningde was much smaller than Shanghai, even smaller than Frankfurt. It was a port town with many piers and boats.

They found a camping store where they bought a few other items they needed. Then they headed to a small metro plaza where they could get on a bus that would stop a couple of miles from the plantation. Shortly after the bus departed, they were out of town and surrounded by forest, heading up into the hills.

The bus eventually dropped them off at a run-down building. There was a small convenience store inside that was open a few hours a day. Still, the building was a holding place for packages and mail sent to and from Ningde and other small cities and villages. A couple of cab drivers familiar with the bus schedule waited for passengers wanting to pay for a ride to another destination.

Sebastian signaled a cab, a beat-up minivan. They traveled slowly on a small, wooded dirt road. In another five minutes, the driver took a right up a long winding incline. Soon, the landscape changed. The thick underbrush and scrub trees that were along the other road were gone. It was slightly darker, with the sun being blocked by a massive tree canopy overhead. The ancient trees were mostly conifers, with huge trunks. Maria sighed audibly in reaction to the majesty of the old growth forest.

Sebastian said, "This is beautiful, isn't it.. The plantation has owned these trees since the 1500s and they have never harvested the wood."

When they finally reached the top, they went through a large wooden gate. At the edge of the forest, just on the other side of the knoll, the vista made Maria catch her breath.

Sebastian asked the driver to stop so Maria could get out and take a picture.

"This is a special valley. You can see it is surrounded by hills and mountains. The valley floor is quite flat, ideal for housing the buildings necessary to run the tea operation and the campground. You can see that most of the valley is surrounded by tea fields that run up and down the hills and even into the mountains in the back."

Maria smelled the burning pine and felt transported to someplace familiar. She smiled. She felt warm, cozy, loved, and confident as a woman. This was thousands of miles away from Germany, yet, she knew she was at home. It was her tea, her plantation, her business. And, there was one more thing; she was in love. With what or whom, she knew not; but she felt as though she had fallen in love.

She glanced at Sebastian. No, she thought, it wasn't him. It was someone else.

She took a few pictures and got back in the car.

Sebastian and Maria were silent as the cab driver drove them down to the campground. He paid and tipped the driver, checked in at the campground kiosk, and soon, they were setting up their tents.

The campsite was just off the valley floor on one end of the campground. Up on a slight knoll, the view was wide open to the remainder of the valley. A small truck was bringing in harvested tea leaves to be dried in one of the smoke houses, and other campers were setting up camp, playing games in the field, or on the playground.

There was plenty of flat ground to set up two tents, far enough apart to make Maria comfortable. On the back side of their campsite the land rose sharply up a mountain. So, they set up the tents to have a view of the valley. The valley was hemmed in by hills and mountains covered with either tea plants or old growth forest. It was the perfect spot to spend the night camping.

After setting up camp, they visited the small shop in the middle of the campground, where they purchased a pendant for Maria and food that would be ready to eat after being warmed over the fire. Sebastian paid to have two stacks of wood dropped off at their site, and the two of them made their way back to their little corner of the plantation.

After finishing their dinner, Maria and Sebastian sat around the fire. Sebastian was pleasant and chatty, but Maria's mind had returned to her dreams and, against her mother's advice, she was in her head, perseverating, rather than relaxing.

However, the campfire did for their conversation what it does for most—it drew Maria into the present and settled her heart. Maria stared into the fire and soon she was remembering the view at the plantation gate, the feeling of returning to someplace warm and special, and she found her voice again as the fire danced and sparks livened up the scene. They discussed their plans for the summer, what they both planned for the future, and where they imagined home would be. The two had much in common as they got to know each other. They shared the same interests, enjoyed the same foods, and both had plans to travel the world.

Maria leaned back on her elbows and looked up at the night sky. As beautiful as the stars were from her apartment balcony, they were much brighter in the middle of the plantation. The night felt ancient, peaceful, comforting, and adventurous. She belonged here.

After spending many hours sitting by the fire, they finally said goodnight at 1 am. Maria thanked Sebastian for inviting her on the trip and climbed into her tent.

Caramel And White

Kai and Hàoyǔ arrived in Hangzhou mid-afternoon the following day. While their pace eventually slowed due to being up all night with no sleep or food, they were able to reach the city with no threat of danger from Yìchén's men.

After a couple of leads, the men were able to find two horses trained for riding and for sale. Kai paid extra for several bowls of rice, bean buns, salted meat, and a change of clothes.

Even with food in their stomachs, the horses proved to be much more rested than their riders. Kai's horse had a uniquely beautiful two-tone coloring; he was pure caramel and white. The mane was distinguished because the top half was white, and the bottom half was caramel.

Kai and Hàoyǔ raced off for Ningde. They decided they needed to get at least eight hours of hard riding before stopping for rest. The trip would take two and a half to three days to complete.

Not much was said while the men were riding. Both of them had a lot on their minds. Their lives had changed entirely in just 24 hours. Hàoyǔ knew that he would never be safe in or around Shanghai again. Kai had made no promises on how long they would remain together. Hàoyǔ acted on a gut feeling he had at the moment. Now, he hoped that Kai would take him under his wing. Whatever Jesus was putting on Kai's heart, Hàoyǔ was hopeful there would be a role he could fulfill.

It had been dark for just over an hour when Kai and Hàoyǔ rode into Ningde from the northeast side. The streets were quiet, so they slowly rode through the village, hoping to find someone who might help.

After a few minutes, they came across a man walking through town in the opposite direction. Hàoyǔ got the man's attention. "Excuse me, sir. We are looking for a place where we might be able to rest for a few hours until the morning. Where might we be able to water the horses and sleep without bothering anyone or intruding on someone's property?"

The man began patting Kai's horse and stroking the front of its neck. "What a beautiful animal. Have you been traveling long?"

"Yes, sir," Hàoyǔ responded. "The horses are just as tired as we are."

"I'm sure," the man responded. "Follow this road through the village. About a mile out, you pass a thick tree line that goes on for miles. Not much moon tonight, but still, you will know it as soon as you see it. Many visitors on horseback stay there overnight. If you go to the side of the tree-line away from the village, you will find a flowing stream perfect for watering your horses. No one will bother you there. The area is well known."

Hàoyǔ gave a bow from on top of his horse. "Thank you, sir, for the help. It is appreciated. Enjoy the rest of your night."

"You as well," the stranger replied before continuing on his way.

Hàoyǔ and Kai found the tree line just as the man had told them they would. In the dark of the night, they could spot several fires spread across a long range, marking where people had made camp for the night.

They stopped to water the horses. "I think it couldn't hurt to get as far from the road as possible," Kai said.

"I second that thought," Hàoyǔ responded. I don't believe we're in any danger of being found. We've put plenty of distance between ourselves and Shanghai. Still, Yìchén and his crew are well known. The last thing we need is for someone to be able to say they saw us here a few days from now."

They found a good spot. Kai had bought a few blankets at a market they had stopped at to water the horses and get lunch the day before.

Once in the dense tree cover, the moonless night was as dark as ink. They dismounted, fumbled in the dark to tie the horses and gather wood for a fire. They eventually had a small fire going, giving them enough light to settle down for the night.

The two men sat on the ground not far from the fire. It felt good to sit peacefully. They were physically and mentally drained, but the chance to sit quietly by the fire was a stronger draw than sleep.

Hàoyǔ broke the fire-lit silence. "What are you thinking about?"

"To be honest, I'm trying not to think." Kai closed his eyes, slowly rotating his neck counterclockwise. "What are you thinking about?" he asked.

"I was hoping you would pray for us again. I don't know how to explain it, but it was relaxing the other night when you prayed after

70

we left Shanghai. I'd like to feel that again right now. And can you explain how that works?"

Kai smiled. "Close your eyes, and bow your head. Maybe take a breath if that helps settle your mind.

"Heavenly Father, we want to take a minute to thank you for who and what you are. Thank you for allowing us to arrive in Ningde safely. We're grateful for the opportunity to finally rest and relax without having to peer over our shoulders in fear of the enemy.

"As grateful as we are for the peace and comfort surrounding us tonight, there is still a lot that's unknown ahead of us. Guide us along our journey, Father, leading us closer to you with everything we do. We surrender both our lives and our will to your glory. Do with us as you will. While Hàoyǔ may not realize it yet, we both love you and wish to be used to advance your kingdom. We pray for this in the name of your Son, Jesus, amen."

Kai leaned back, applying the weight of his upper body on his elbows against the ground. He thought to himself for a few seconds and began ministering to Hàoyǔ.

"Prayer is our direct line of communication to Jesus and God the Father. Therefore, it must be the most important conversation in our daily lives. Without prayer, it's difficult for us to follow the will of God and the purposes He has for us."

"What's the difference between Jesus and God the Father," Hàoyǔ asked. "If Jesus is the God of the Christian faith, why do you pray to this God the Father?"

Kai cleared his throat and sat up straighter. The Triune God was foreign to Asian religions. Kai had struggled with the concept himself

71

at first. So, he decided to introduce God the Father, the Creator. Every nation knows about its Creator.

"Hàoyŭ," Kai began, "the Creator made the world we live in and everything in it. What is the Creator's name in your language?"

"Shang Di," Hàoyŭ said.

"Great," Kai responded. "Japan's is Amenominakanushi. And the Bible calls Him several other names; Yahweh, El Shaddai, and El Elyon to name a few. He is the benevolent, uncreated Creator of all things. The Bible says that after giving form and shape to the world, our Heavenly Father created the waters of the seas. He formed the land we live on, made light of the day and darkness of the night. He made every star in the sky and knows each of them by name.

"Once He made everything in the world, He created man in His image. Did you catch that?" Kai asked. "God the Father *made* the world and everything in it, but He *created* man in His image."

Hàoyŭ was gazing up at a single star he could see between the tree canopy leaves. After a few moments of silence, he had to know more. "What is the difference between making something and creating it?" he asked.

"Everything that the Father made, He was able to think into existence," Kai explained. "He was able to have a thought, and something formed out of nothing. So, God the Father thought the world we live in into existence."

"With man, it was different," Kai continued. "The Father formed the first man out of the dust of the ground. He formed the shell of a man. Then, when everything was perfect, God bent down facing the shell of the man and breathed the breath of life into Adam, the first man.

Adam opened his eyes for the first time and was face-to-face with his Creator. Adam was breathing the very breath of God."

"How is Jesus involved?" Hàoyǔ asked.

"That is a question for another day," Kai answered. "I would like to have the tea room scrolls and the Bible open in front of us before going any further. A fresh mind will also go a long way in understanding a Triune God.

"Let's get some sleep now. For tonight, think about you and your Creator God and how you might live in His plan for you. You aren't an accident or the result of a random act, Hàoyǔ. You were created by a loving God who loves you specifically and has a special plan and purpose for your life. Your dad knew it was terrific to *live in sync with His plan*, rather than ignoring or fighting it."

Kai stood up and grabbed two pieces of wood from the small pile they had gathered. He maneuvered the already burning logs and then laid the two additional pieces across the top.

After Kai laid down to sleep, he prayed silently. "I'm ready for this, Father. I'm a little afraid, but I have faith in you. You wouldn't have brought me this far for me to fail now. Guide me, Father. Be my strength when I have none. Lead me when I am lost. Be my comfort when I'm unable to find any on my own. I trust you and know things are going as you have planned. Thank you, God."

Kai woke early and ventured down to the small creek through the thicket. There he found an isolated place where he could be by himself in prayer.

The quiet allowed Kai to connect with the Holy Spirit. After spending around an hour in prayer and with his Bible, Kai felt alive. His spirit was refreshed. Nobumasa had taught him the value of "sabbath-ing," entering God's rest at all times, not just once a week, *"for whoever has entered God's rest has also rested from his works as God did from his."* (Heb 4:10).

In this mindset, Nobumasa had taught him, we are not necessarily resting from physical work. Instead, God gives us rest in the form of *confidence that His work **will** be done through us.* It is restful to know that God already has plans to accomplish His work through us and that He will do it! Our part is to simply live in close contact with Him, obedient to His voice and Word. He does everything else. Jesus modeled this frequently through time alone with God the Father. Time alone keeps us attentive to His will, voice, and ways.

After Hàoyǔ had woken, Kai prayed over him.

The day ahead seemed simple enough. Ride back to Ningde. Discretely get directions to the plantation. Ride to the plantation.

Little did either of them know that God's real journey was just beginning.

"How much information do you have on this plantation?" Kai asked.

"I'll be honest, not a lot," Hàoyǔ replied. "I know it is quite a few miles outside the village and not easy to find. Supposedly, locals know where it is. A woman owns it. Normally either she or one of her closest people will talk with the person looking for refuge. Then they decide if the plantation is a good fit for them."

Kai looked at Hàoyǔ directly. "We are in an awkward predicament. We need refuge but don't want anyone to know or remember us if Yìchén comes looking for us. Yet, to find refuge, we must ask where it is, revealing our needs and making ourselves more memorable.

This is where we trust our Heavenly Father. We take action and depend on Him for results. Let's go to the village, find some breakfast, and trust God will lead us to ask the *right* local."

Ningde seemed like a warm and welcome place. Most people were smiling and greeted each other with a few kind words.

Kai and Hàoyǔ found a small place where they could eat some eggs and rice for breakfast. They tied their horses in front of the building and sat at a public table. A teenage girl approached the table, bowing to show respect to the two men. She took their order and brought their food to them several minutes later.

Halfway through the meal, the girl appeared again, asking if Kai and Hàoyǔ enjoyed their food and if they needed anything else.

Kai's tea was superb. It had an unusual smoky flavor. "This tea is delicious," he told her. "What's your secret?"

The young girl's smile showed she was used to questions and comments about the brew.

"Our secret is that everything is local," the girl replied with a smile. "The tea leaves are grown on my friend's plantation in the hills west of the village. We only buy tea leaves from her. The plantation plays a role in employing locals in need of work. People come from all over to buy her special tea leaves."

Kai smiled and thanked her again.

Kai and Hàoyǔ finished their meal and paid the bill. The girl greeted them one last time on their way out, thanking them for coming in.

"I'm just curious," Kai asked her on their way out. "If I wanted to buy some more of your friend's tea, where could I find her plantation?"

The young girl enthusiastically gave Kai directions to the plantation. They could be there on a horse in around an hour. Kai would have to pay attention to detail as they traveled, though. The plantation was well off the popular trails. There were tree lines to look for and wagon trails that weren't easily visible.

An hour later, about the time they were already supposed to be there, Kai was pretty sure they were lost.

Kai and Hàoyǔ brought their horses to a complete stop. They sat on their horses, looking at a long narrow bridge that crossed a raging river. Old and missing some planks, it seemed unlikely to lead to the plantation. But, it was the only choice they had.

Hàoyǔ broke the silence, "My mother used to say: 'Some bridges are not meant to be crossed.'"

"I can't help but think we've taken a wrong turn somewhere," Kai said. "The girl at breakfast was very descriptive with her directions. She would have mentioned the bridge if we were supposed to cross it. But, we followed her directions perfectly."

Kai climbed down from his horse and walked to the bridge. There was a wide gate leading to the bridge, which seemed odd, given that the bridge was narrow, barely wide enough to fit a single horse.

Kai remembered his brother telling him that the main verse on each scroll contained one of just five top teachings of Jesus Christ. At the top of the south scroll was the verse, *"Enter by the narrow gate. For the gate is wide and the way is easy that leads to destruction, and those who enter by it are many. For the gate is narrow and the way is hard that leads to life, and those who find it are few." Matthew 7:13-14*

Gates were significant in Japan and China. They marked entry points, both physical and metaphysical. Kai wondered if this wide gate and narrow path were meaningful to the builder.

He picked up a rock from the trail and tossed it into the rapids below the bridge. The river was far too deep and treacherous to cross on horseback and at least seventy feet wide.

The bridge was in rough shape. In addition to some boards missing, others appeared weak. Kai slowly walked about fifteen feet across the bridge by himself. He jumped up and down twice. The bridge seemed more robust than it looked.

"Your choice," Kai said to his companion. "Would you like to cross first or follow after me? I don't think we should have both horses on the bridge simultaneously. I'm happy to cross first to test it."

"Okay," Hàoyǔ answered.

Kai got off of his horse and slowly walked it across the bridge. One of the horse's legs broke through a board in a couple of places. But each time, luckily, the other three legs held, and eventually, Kai and his horse made it safely across the bridge.

Hàoyǔ, a skilled horseman, had not dismounted. He watched Kai's horse slowly damage the bridge; from his point of view, it seemed that a running horse would be safer. With speed, each board needed less time to hold up, and a running horse is adept at avoiding gaps.

Hàoyǔ held the reins in one hand and wrapped the horse's mane around his fingers. He jammed his feet into the horse's side, sending the animal across the bridge at full speed.

Just as Hàoyǔ had surmised, the horse adeptly flew over the missing planks, and didn't punch through any others. His plan was working.

About three-quarters of the way across the bridge, there was a structural tower in the river. As the horse galloped toward it, Kai watched the pylon loosen and crumble. Rock, dirt, and wood underneath gave way, and Hàoyǔ and his horse dropped twenty feet into the rapids below.

Kai saw his friend drop into the raging river. He monitored the surface for signs of life. The horse came up first, neighing frantically. By the time Hàoyǔ came up for air, he was fifty feet downstream. He got one breath before he crashed into a boulder, bounced right, and was forced under again.

Kai mounted his horse, turned, and raced down the only path available, hoping it would bank left and follow the stream. It didn't. The road stayed straight, heading away from the river. Kai rode for a mile to see if he could reach an intersection. Nothing.

Desperate now, he turned and rode back to the river. He tied up his horse at the river and was determined to follow the stream by foot. Kai hoped that Hàoyǔ was pushed to the bank of the river and quickly made it out of the stream. Kai prayed he would find him alive.

Kai's progress downstream was slow. Next to the stream, the bushes were thick, and the boulders were large. Kai's emotions were raw as he watched the stream rush along at twenty times his pace. His only hope would be for Hàoyǔ to have escaped the rapids quickly.

Otherwise, he would be miles down the stream before Kai made it a hundred yards.

Kai persevered. He called out for Hàoyǔ every ten yards or so, praying all the while.

Six hours later, scratched, bruised, and hungry, Kai gave up and turned back. With just a couple of hours of daylight left, he knew he was not going to find Hàoyǔ that night.

It was well after dark when he finally made it back to the collapsed bridge. The return trip had been more difficult in the moonlight. He stepped on a boulder, and it turned under his foot. His ankle twisted, and his foot slipped off. At that exact moment, his foot fell into a crevasse, and the boulder rolled against it crashing into the next rock, smashing his ankle.

He managed to dislodge his foot, but both bones were fractured. When he raised his foot, it flopped uncontrollably.

He had to crawl an excruciating half mile out of the woods. When he finally recognized the path to the bridge, he rejoiced, knowing it was time to water his horse, eat, and bed down for the remainder of the night.

He expected to hear his horse knicker when he got close.

Instead, it was eerily silent, like the eye of the storm.

When he got to the tree where he had tied his horse, his horse was gone.

It's You!

The photo album lying in the woods looked familiar. It was the same one that was in the room with no doors or windows. She immediately skipped to the back where she'd read the letter telling her this would be the summer that transformed the rest of her life.

The letter was gone. Instead, Maria found new images in the album.

Pictures were taken throughout the day, starting with an image of her eating rice rolls at the coffee shop. Several pictures were during the train ride, followed by the trip in the van to the plantation, and then photos from the walk through the campground they had taken before eating dinner. Maria noticed one characteristic in common. Sebastian wasn't included in any of the pictures. It was as if he was a ghost who couldn't be photographed, visible only to her.

Maria made it to the last page of the photo album. The front of the page had no photo, but a beautiful drawing of a wooden cross standing on the ground in front of an old building made from wooden planks and bamboo. The drawing had exquisite detail and looked as if it were hundreds of years old.

Maria anxiously flipped the last page to see if anything was on the back. In the middle of the page was a drawing made with colored pencils. It was of Maria sitting on the train holding the pendant from Sebastian's necklace in her hand. Someone had written something in small letters right underneath the drawing. Maria picked up the photo album and held it closer to her face to determine what the words were.

"Welcome home, Maria. There is much to learn and a lot to be done. Get ready for wisdom and transformation."

Maria awoke and sat bolt upright. She scrambled out of the sleeping bag, unzipped the nylon tent and crawled outside on her hands and knees. Maria was gasping for breath. She'd never had a panic attack, but she felt this must be one. Maria stood to her feet, and looked back at the view of the valley. It was calming, like a lavender bubble bath.

She looked around at Sebastian's tent and listened for any stirrings from. Hearing nothing, she assumed he was asleep. She even tiptoed over and peaked in his window. He was asleep. Thank goodness.

She retrieved her backpack and phone out of the tent. It was a few minutes after 6:00 a.m. She had climbed into the tent to sleep just over five hours ago.

Wide awake now, she quietly sat at the picnic table and took out her computer to record the dream. She wrote out the details and her emotions—from seeing the pendant for the first time around Sebastian's neck to Sebastian being missing from the photos to the message that repeated the warning to "get ready."

With Sebastian still not stirring, she decided to shower and get dressed for the day. The restroom pavilion was a short walk in the center of the campground.

Maria stood under the shower-head with her eyes closed, reliving the dream she'd just had. "Welcome home, Maria. There is much to learn and a lot to be done. Get ready for wisdom and transformation."

How could this be home? On top of that, what would she learn and be doing? There was significance with the pendant. Was that the wisdom and transformation? How did the plantation tie into everything?

Maria dried off and dressed. She brushed her teeth and spent a few minutes brushing her hair. After putting on a little makeup, Maria headed out of the pavilion building to make her way back to the campsite.

Maria was ready to talk. She was stuck in her head, replaying the dream repeatedly. She needed to process these dreams with someone, hoping she could do that with Sebastian.

Maria looked to the right and noticed that the small shop in the center of the campground was already open. A hot cup of tea, she thought. That would taste good.

Maria stepped up to the counter.

"What can I help you with?" a friendly middle-aged woman asked behind the counter.

"I would like a hot tea, please," Maria asked.

"Would you like a cup of our famous seasoned by fire tea?"

"That sounds great," Maria said. "Make it two. I have a friend who is still at our campsite."

"It will be just a few minutes. We fresh brew each cup," the woman replied. "You can walk around the store or even wait outside if you'd like, and someone will bring it out."

"Thank you," Maria said as she paid the bill and walked outside.

The campground was beginning to wake up and come to life. Campers were stirring and making their way to and from the shower and restroom pavilion. Maria sat on a chair just outside the door. She watched as two squirrels chased each other around a tree before one of them took off for their nest. Even nature was getting started with the new day.

"Two cups of seasoned by fire tea," a cheerful voice said, approaching Maria from behind.

She stood up from her chair and turned towards the gentleman who had called out her order. Maria's mouth dropped at what she saw.

The gentleman was a few inches taller than Maria. He had short, perfectly combed, gray hair. The smile on his face lit up like the morning sun. He spoke like his intent was to comfort and encourage with every word he said. It was a familiar voice, one Maria had heard on two different occasions.

She was looking at the older man from the one-room shack in her dreams.

"It's you," Maria said just loud enough for the man to hear. "How is this happening?" Maria asked.

She looked down and whispered, "Is this another dream?"

"I'm sorry?" the man replied with a measured kindness. "I couldn't make out what you were saying. Is everything alright?"

"What is going on?" Maria asked, a little louder this time.

"Did you order two cups of seasoned by fire tea?" the man asked, standing just a few feet away.

"I can't believe it. It's you!" Maria said.

The man turned around to see if Maria was addressing someone else.

"Ma'am, I am pleased to see you too, but forgive me for not remembering the connection."

"Please," Maria quickly said, "tell me your name before I wake up. I must know what to call you," she continued.

"My name is Hu." He bowed slightly to Maria. "I have met many people in my long life. Please forgive my rudeness for not knowing your name."

Maria was in shock. She was positive this was the man from her dream and that she had bumped into him for a reason.

"How can you say that after the previous two times we talked?" Maria asked. "What is it you are supposed to be teaching me?"

The last question got Hu's attention. Perhaps she had been a student. Over the past forty-five years, he taught the Bible via the Tea Room Scrolls to hundreds of people. Now in his late sixties, teaching God's Word had been his life's work.

"Is this another dream?" Maria's demand seemed odd and out of context.

"Here, why don't we sit down," he said while pointing over at a picnic table. He touched her arm gently to lead her over.

The touch brought comfort and grounding to a dazed Maria. And it assured her she was not in a dream. This was real.

But the comfort lasted only seconds as she re-lived the embarrassment of the wake up from the nightmare on the flight to Shanghai. The last few days had disoriented her; her dreams seemed as if they were real life, and reality seemed like a dream. It was too much.

"I'm sorry," Maria whispered, fighting back the tears. "I thought you were someone else. I must get going," she continued as she took the two cups of tea from the gentleman.

"Wait, let's talk about this for a few minutes," he interrupted.

"I have to go," Maria continued. "My friend is waiting for me back at our campsite. We're getting ready to leave soon."

Maria took the tea and walked away quickly. She wanted to get as far away from the scene as she could. Maybe even leave the plantation right away. But, she thought, Sebastian would not understand, so she would have to explain to him, but then he still wouldn't understand, because *nobody could understand this.*

Better to leave it inside myself and not tell anyone, she resolved. Nobody should know.

Yet, as soon as she decided she wouldn't talk about it, her hands started shaking as if all the emotion needed to come out. Her hands felt like they were going to explode.

She slowed her pace to avoid spilling the tea. But the hand tremor traveled to her arms. Her head had been looking down at the ground, confident that looking up would engage more stimulation than she could handle.

With her body trembling, she stopped walking and set the cups down. Adrenaline was rushing through her veins. She stood looking at the ground, silently asking the soil to absorb the excess energy panicking her muscles.

Finding no relief, Maria lifted her head and peered across the horizon toward her campsite. Birds were flying in and out of the woods. The bright morning sun was dancing off the dew-covered grass, casting massive shadows behind the trees in the field. The sky was azure blue. Scattered across the area were the smiling faces of orange-red poppies greeting the sun, "Good morning, life is fabulous."

Her heart slowed as she soaked in the glory she was witnessing.

From this distance, Sebastian's tent appeared undisturbed. Maybe she should wake him and talk? It would be good to talk. Beyond their tents, a trail disappeared into the woods.

Days ago, her lilly-white life had no color, no passion, nothing to live for. She had cried out to the universe to give her something beyond a pale existence. Had she cried too loud?

As if her mind knew the answer and she didn't, she suddenly became aware of where she was. It was the scene that surrounded the shack in her dreams.

Maria took a few steps back to take in the scene from a further distance. She couldn't believe what she was seeing. The exact angle and corners as their site sat against the woods. The same steep hill behind and a path around the right. It was a picture-perfect vision of what she'd seen in the dream. This was where the older man brought her a cup of tea, dropped it, and then picked up the pendant and placed it in Maria's hand.

The revelation and the beauty of the scene, mixed with an of ethereal wispiness, stopped the trembling. But her mind still felt like she was in a fog of malcontent. There was nothing physically wrong with her, she wasn't in any danger, but the disorientation of reality vs. dream left her confused, weak, and wanting to flee.

She walked toward the campsite, still not knowing what she would do when she got there.

"There you are," Sebastian called out. "I was starting to get worried after realizing you weren't in your tent."

Maria silently walked the rest of the distance to the fire pit on the campsite and handed Sebastian one of the cups of tea.

"I have to get out of here," Maria quickly blurted out. "I must get back to Shanghai as quickly as possible."

"What are you talking about?" Sebastian asked. "Is everything alright?"

"No, it's not," Maria replied. "I'm sorry, Sebastian. There's been a family emergency. I have to return to Shanghai as quickly as possible and might need to go home to Frankfurt for a few days. I'll buy the new train tickets, pay for the bus and cab, whatever I need to. I just have to get back as soon as I can."

"Let's pack our stuff," Sebastian replied as if the change of plans was no inconvenience. "Part of the rental fee for the tents is that they come and take them down, so they have an opportunity to make sure they are clean and sterile. All we have to do is check out at the shop and tell them we are leaving."

While they packed up, Maria decided she should accompany Sebastian as he checked out at the store. Maria hoped to see the older man again—maybe she had made it all up, perhaps the overwhelming emotions she was experiencing would go away if he wasn't the man from her dreams.

They entered the small shop and walked to the counter. After thoroughly examining the shop, Maria couldn't see either the woman who had taken her order or the gentleman who brought her the two cups of tea. Instead, this time, a young man was behind the counter who was about their age.

After buying a few drinks and snacks for the train ride, Maria returned to the pavilion to use the restroom while they waited for a cab. She freshened up in the mirror, calmed herself the best she could, and then headed out the door to return to where Sebastian was waiting.

"Excuse me, miss?" Maria turned her head towards the voice calling after her. "Hu gave me this card and asked if I would give it to you if I saw you again. He owns the campground and brought you the tea you ordered this morning. He wrote his cell number on the back. Hu wanted me to tell you that he is sorry for this morning and hopes you will give him a call. He said it is important."

"Thank you," Maria said as she took the card from the woman. It was a plantation business card with contact information for the campground. Maria flipped it over and in precise handwriting was a phone number and the name 'Hu Oda.'

"Is Hu still around?" Maria looked up. But the woman had left as quickly as she arrived.

Few Find It

Oh, Lord God, have mercy on me."

Kai had no horse, food, clothing, bedding, or money. And perhaps worst of all, the tea room scrolls were gone.

He was lost in the inner recesses of China with little else but the clothes on his back, his sanity, and the Holy Spirit.

He sat down in the dark and wondered why he had ever left the sea. He was prepared for and lived through nearly every situation imaginable at sea. He knew what to do. Worthy and loyal men surrounded him, and he was confident at sea.

Now, on land, he was lost, adrift, lonely, and anything but confident.

As he thought about his plight, he realized he had to make one move at a time. And the *only rational* next move was to sleep.

Furthermore, he resolved to sleep on the trail. A man with money would hide in the woods to sleep. A lost man with nothing to lose sleeps where he might be found.

"Heavenly Father, may I be found!"

The morning sun arose, bearing disappointment. Nobody had traveled by, and Kai's ankle had swollen with an inch thick casing.

The three-inch gash on his thigh was oozing and painful, and his back and neck were sore from the hard ground.

He lay on the ground listening. The only sound was an angry river that had taken his ally and spoke no hope into a broken man's heart.

He tried to stand up, praying that a miracle had happened while he slept. Not so. His ankle collapsed in agony when he put the slightest weight on it.

He assessed the situation. He knew the trail was deserted for at least a mile. It was unknown how much further he would have to crawl to see any chance of life. And he knew he could not go back over the bridge because it was destroyed.

He sat back down and thought logically. Kai felt that people must travel on this path, and sooner or later, someone would come to one side of the river or the other. If he stayed at the river's edge, he could be found by people on both sides; whereas leaving the bridge would cut his chances in half.

Decided, he crawled down to the river. He drank heartily, rinsed his wounds, and stuck his ankle in the cold water to bring down the swelling. Then he crawled back up the bank and sat on the end of the bridge.

He settled in for the wait. Indeed, he thought, someone would be by soon.

He smiled as he thought about what his brother would say. Nobumasa had been exiled on a remote mountain in the cold of northern Japan. He had nearly died that first winter.

Nobumasa had said. "It was just God and me. And *everyone* should reach a time in their life when it is just them and their Creator. Total reliance on God is what He wants, but few of us ever really get tested."

Kai looked skyward, "It's just you and me. Help me pass this test. I'm yours, Father, do with me as you will."

The following days passed with little to celebrate. Each morning the sun rose bearing more disappointment. He drank water, ate raw grass by the riverside, and waited.

The nights were cold, and the days were warm. It rained several times, watering a tea plantation that he could only imagine in his mind and drenching his wasting body lying limp on a remote path in China.

The first days he tracked by marking lines on the dirt path. But as days passed by and Kai grew weaker from lack of food, he lost count. He remembered only one thing: part of the south scroll, which he repeated throughout the day. *The gate is narrow and the way is hard that leads to life, and those who find it are few.*

One day the sun rose to bear a gift.

"What did you say?" The man bent over Kai, lightly touching him on the shoulder.

Kai was delirious, incapable of answering the question. He repeated a single phrase, "Few find it. But I found it. Thank you, Jesus."

"Find what, sir?"

Kai didn't hear or respond; he just repeated, "Few find it."

A Waiter Left Waiting

The return trip to Shanghai was quiet for the most part. Sebastian wasn't sure what to say, and he could see that Maria's mind was elsewhere. She had told him that there was a family emergency at home but didn't offer any other details. He couldn't help but wonder if she would remember the fun the two had together the night before.

Sebastian waved down a taxi for Maria once they got off the train in Shanghai. Refusing to allow her to pay, he handed the driver enough cash to cover taking Maria to her apartment. She took him by the hand and kissed his cheek.

"Thank you for understanding," she whispered. "Last night was one that I will cherish. I'm so glad that the two of us met."

"Text me when you get home, so I know that you made it okay," he told her.

Maria climbed into the cab and headed for her apartment.

After almost eight hours of *uninterrupted* sleep, Maria woke up fresh and ready to discover Shanghai the following day. It was the first time she'd slept without being awakened by a dream since boarding the plane to leave Frankfurt.

The next several days were spent touring Shanghai. She enjoyed her city living with no dreams causing distraction, sleep deprivation, and confusion.

She visited the café once to see Sebastian. She knew she was leaving Sebastian for good without giving him a full explanation. She didn't understand it herself, let alone try to explain it to him. She knew it wouldn't work with Sebastian. She couldn't open up to him about her confused state of mind. But she also knew he deserved to know it was her, not him. She didn't want to let him think he was the cause of her difficulty. She told him, "My stuff I'm going through is a little better, though tenuous."

In all, she had seven nights of great sleep.

It was fun to explore a new city, but Maria was a go-getter, energetic, and ready for an adventure or a problem to solve. Her days started to drag. She was beginning to get bored again. A new city was fun for a while, but where is the purpose, dynamism, and change-maker results in exploring a city? 'Nowhere' was the answer.

She started to feel listless again, like she had in Germany. She was trapped within the walls; Chinese walls were just as hopeless, depressing, and passionless as German walls.

Maria went to sleep that night asking again for an escape, a way outside the white-washed walls of a wonderfully mediocre, inexcusably apathetic existence.

In the dream, Maria was lost somewhere deep in the middle of a forest. While she couldn't see anyone, Maria felt someone was pursuing her. She'd been running for hours. Regardless of how far or fast she went, Maria could not flee from whoever was chasing her.

She crouched down next to a tree, trying to hide. Without knowing the direction of her pursuer, she couldn't determine what side of the tree was best to hide. After circling the tree three times, she realized she must run again. As she stepped away from the tree, Hu appeared.

"There is way, a Tao, you know not of," he whispered. "I will show you the way. If you had called me when you returned home, maybe you wouldn't be in this state of indecision."

Hu took a few steps in the opposite direction Maria was planning to take. "Come on," he continued. "Now is the time. Now is the day."

Maria opened her eyes and sat up on the edge of the bed. The dreams were back. Before going to sleep, she asked for a way out of the monochrome prison. She wanted vibrancy of meaning and passion. And once again, she had received answers.

She re-read her previous journal entries and realized there was a common thread: peace was obtainable, but in reality *she* was fearful and indecisive. She wanted more from life, but she was afraid. She asked for an answer, got a partial solution. Yet every time, she awoke in fear and needing to flee.

After reading over her entries that included the older man, Maria compared them to her latest dream. Hu seemed to know exactly where she needed to go.

Maria went to the living room and dug through her backpack, looking for the business card with Hu's number. She grabbed her phone and headed for the chair on the balcony. The afternoon noise seemed quieter than usual.

She punched the numbers and hesitated. What if, she thought. What if he thinks I'm crazy?

Out loud to the traffic below, she said, "I'm not crazy, and I'm not afraid."

She pressed the green phone symbol.

"Hello," a voice answered after the third ring.

"Hi, is this Hu?"

"Yes, it is. May I ask who I'm speaking with?" he replied.

"This is Maria. I'm the person you brought the two cups of tea out to last week at the campground. A woman gave me a card with your number before I left."

"I remember," he told her. "I've been hoping you would call. I apologize for my rudeness when we met."

"No, it's alright," Maria interrupted. "I'm the one who should be apologizing. The two of us had never met before."

"It seems you are looking for something, Maria. And I may know where you will find it. Is this true that you are looking for something?"

Maria explained how she needed to escape what she viewed as a boring life in Germany and find passion by exploring the world. She didn't know what she was trying to find, but she hoped there was more to life.

"You mentioned something about knowing me from dreams. Can you explain?"

Maria told him everything, starting with her nightmare on the flight to Shanghai. She told Hu about the shack in the woods and described both the inside and outside. Next, Maria recounted the wisdom and transformation she was supposed to be looking for and how the cup of tea magically turned into the pendant representing the wisdom and transformation.

"Does any of this make sense to you at all?" Maria finally asked.

Hu cleared his throat.

"It might. But first, let me say you may not be ready for my answer. These dreams seem to have upset you, Maria. I like to say that fear comes in with the kaleidoscope."

Maria was silent.

Hu continued. "Let me explain. When things are well, we have no fear but suffer malaise. In the malaise, we seek passion, which is the kaleidoscope. But the passion of the kaleidoscope brings partial answers, shapes, and shadows. Which in turn can trigger fear."

Hu was silent a moment. Maria didn't fill in the silence, but her mind was thinking, 'He's right! This is what I've been experiencing. The malaise, the desire for more, and then the fear of the kaleidoscope!

"Are you truly seeking more?" he finally asked.

Maria wavered. She wasn't sure she should answer that question from a man she didn't know. What if he was in a cult? What if…

Maria knew the answer. She wanted more. She was still afraid of what she would find but *knew she wanted more.*

Furthermore as she let the silence lengthen, she felt peace coming over the phone; something was settling in her heart that Hu was trustworthy.

"Yes," she finally said.

A Toy Boat Rescue

Hàoyŭ saw the pylon crumbling as he was approaching it. Everything was in slow motion. He knew he was in trouble but thought he might still make it all the way, given his speed.

He made it past the tower, but shortly after that, the bridge collapsed under the stampeding horse. Had the bridge fallen flat, Hàoyŭ might have made it the next twenty feet. But the bridge collapsed unevenly, leaning downstream. Hàoyŭ and the horse hit the foaming water flat on their sides. As they fell, Hàoyŭ thought, "God, I still want to know you. Please save me."

He submerged immediately, letting go of the reins and sliding off the saddle. He came up to the surface, but the water was churning, rolling, and spraying. He gulped for air but choked on the mix of air and water. His shoulder and rib cage slammed into a boulder, knocking the remaining air out of him and bouncing him further into the middle of the rapids. He took a panicked breath and managed to get only air, no water. After another full breath, he spun around to see downstream and put his legs in front of him, reasoning that it was better to hit a boulder with his legs than his head.

He had a good run for a while, missing every boulder as the stream tossed him over and around the stones in the stream. And he rejoiced when he saw that the rapids would end soon.

He was positioned perfectly with his legs ahead of him for the final rapids. But he didn't see the ten-foot drop at the end; it was like the rapid's last hurrah.

Suddenly, the bottom dropped out, and he flew down the ten-foot drop, smashing his left leg into a boulder. He heard the crack of bone as it splintered under pressure. Then his body spun right and smashed his right shoulder into another boulder.

The muscle contraction around his broken leg immediately shortened the leg, shoving the bone fragments into places they shouldn't. Hàoyǔ had never experienced this level of pain.

He lost consciousness. The river was still flowing fast, sweeping him downstream. But the water's surface was calm, so he floated on his back, still breathing.

Humanity was never designed for amphibious travel. Natural flotation is face down for humans. In his unconscious state, he started to list to the left, and just as his mouth submerged, he awoke. He sucked in water and panicked. He fought to maneuver onto his back, choking and sputtering. Every movement, including the coughing, caused excruciating pain.

But he was glad to be alive. He cleared his lungs finally and used his one good arm to steady himself in the fast-moving current. His mind cleared enough to start focusing on getting out of the river. He used his left arm to make some slow progress in steering toward the bank.

He could see a large boulder sticking out of the water a long way ahead. It was not far from the shoreline, so he determined that if he could get in its path and hit the boulder with his good leg, he could push himself off toward shore. It was a risky plan because if he crashed his broken leg, he was likely to faint again and may not survive this time.

But, with little to propel him toward shore, and his one good arm on the wrong side of his body, he couldn't see any other way to get out of the river. He needed a way to shove himself into the bank and hopefully beach himself enough to grab something with his good arm.

As he approached the boulder, he prayed, "God, I know I have not been your friend. But if you are real, I need you now more than ever. If you can help me out now, I promise I will study, learn and be the man you want me to be."

Before he hit the boulder, his left leg glanced over another rock below the surface. He cried out in anguish. But it was just the right change in momentum; his right leg spun into the boulder, and Hàoyǔ's right foot landed squarely. He shoved with all his might and jettisoned himself into the river bank. He flipped over, crying out in pain. He desperately grasped at the sand and roots as his legs started to be swept away by the current.

He found a solid root with his good arm and pulled with all his might. He managed to get himself far enough out of the water to know he was safe, and with feet still dangling in the water, he slipped out of consciousness.

That afternoon, a blacksmith's son went to the river to float a miniature raft he had made out of dried bamboo. He saw "a dead man," yelled, and got his father to retrieve him out of the river.

Hàoyǔ woke up in a bed of straw the following day. He was in the loft in the blacksmith's barn. It was the only place the family had to take in a guest. Plus, it was warm due to being above the blacksmith's furnace.

The oldest daughter mostly attended to Hàoyǔ, but the blacksmith and his wife came up, too, to help and encourage him.

Hàoyǔ needed the encouragement. He feared he would never walk again. As the days passed, he made little progress toward walking.

Lying on his back, unable to get up and with only his thoughts to pass the time, he assumed that Kai had given him up for dead. He didn't know Kai had sacrificed to try and find him; and, at that very moment, was lying alone on a small dirt path, slipping towards death.

It's a lonely feeling, being left behind. Hàoyǔ felt this same feeling when his father had been murdered. Year's later, in a private conversation with a Christian missionary, Hàoyǔ had confided his emotions about losing his dad. The missionary confirmed that his dad had indeed been a Christian, "But," he said, "God the Father pursues us, each of us, tracking us down in the deepest alleyways and the darkest recesses of life. The further we retreat, stumble or fall, the more miraculous the rescue becomes. Hàoyǔ, God will be with you and rescue you one day. He has plans for you, son."

Hàoyǔ silently prayed. "Maybe I didn't need Kai to rescue me. Maybe I just need you. Please God, help me."

One day, Hàoyǔ confided in the blacksmith regarding the events leading up to the fall. It felt good to confess. He told him about being hired to maim and rob Kai, Kai's mission, including the tea room scrolls, his sudden change of mind in the middle of the robbery, the flight out of Shanghai, the pursuit of the tea plantation, getting lost, and the fateful crossing of the old rickety bridge.

The blacksmith knew about the tea plantation; it was at least ten miles from them. The blacksmith was unfamiliar with the bridge, but he knew it was several miles upstream because he knew where the rapids were. Everyone knew the rapids; they were unnavigable. Those traveling by river had to portage around the rapids. Hàoyǔ had not only flown down them in a free fall but floated on his back with a shattered leg and torn shoulder for a long time. It was a miracle he was alive and could beach himself on the river bank.

Hàoyǔ slept a lot those first two weeks. But he was often awakened by the clanging of iron sharpening and shaping iron and by customers coming in to discuss projects.

One day he overheard a man talking to the blacksmith about a new sword. He could tell they knew each other and that the man had previously only asked for the most basic blacksmith work. But now, he indicated that he had come into an inheritance and wanted a ceremonial sword.

"That's good for you; was it a relative who left you money?"

"Yes, my uncle, and he left me this beautiful horse."

The blacksmith walked a few steps toward the entrance. "Yes, my friend, beautiful coloring and that mane! I've never seen a two-toned mane, white up top and light brown on the bottom."

Hàoyǔ's heart skipped. He scooted up onto his hands to see out the window. Down below was Kai's horse. He waited until the man left to talk to the blacksmith.

"You remember the man I saved and traveled with? That horse outside today was his horse! How well do you know the man who came today? Is he an honest man?"

"I know him very well. We have both lived in this village our whole lives. And, no, he is not an honest man. He is a drinker, not a reliable worker, and has barely subsisted most of his adult life. The villagers have often supported his family when he was irresponsible with his money."

Hàoyǔ and the blacksmith hatched a plan to recover Kai's goods. The blacksmith invited him over for drinks the next day "to celebrate his inheritance." When he was slightly drunk, the blacksmith told him that he knew the horse was stolen. And he proved it by telling him that the horse was carrying five unique scrolls.

"You are going to turn these goods over to my recovering patient, or I will tell the townspeople. Horse thievery is a capital offense. Do you want to hang or return everything? Which will it be?"

It was not a difficult choice. The thief chose to return Kai's possessions.

With Kai's goods recovered, Hàoyǔ made better progress in his physical and emotional health. It was comforting to Hàoyǔ to know Kai probably did not give up on finding him. Kai had *also* fallen to demise. He hoped Kai was okay, wherever he was.

With the money that was recovered, Hàoyǔ hired a local man, whom the blacksmith trusted, to go upstream and see if he could find Kai. He instructed the man to find the collapsed bridge and then go to the tea plantation. And if he found Kai, let him know that Hàoyǔ was alive and would join him at the plantation as soon as possible...*with the scrolls!*

Facing The Kaleidoscope

Hu was at the train station in Ningde when Maria arrived. Unlike the first visit with Sebastian, Maria brought much more for this trip. She had her backpack, as well as a large suitcase. In the forty-eight hours since the first phone call with Hu, Maria had decided to keep an open mind about how long she would stay at the campground. She was prepared to be gone for up to two weeks.

Hu bowed low when he greeted Maria.

In a good mood, Maria returned the bow but quickly insisted on a hug. Hu embraced her like a grandfather, with warmth and welcome. Maria suddenly felt she was returning to where she belonged. It was a long hug in which Hu let Maria decide how long to let it linger. When she finally let go, Hu saw Maria quickly wipe a tear from her cheek.

"Is everything alright?" he asked.

"Yes, I'm fine," Maria assured him.

"But you have a tear?"

"I don't know," Maria admitted. "I have had this feeling the past two days that life as I know it is about to change. It's as if I'm going to discover something important."

"Does this frighten you?" Hu asked as the two of them made their way to his truck.

"Yes," Maria said. "Though maybe the word is nervous. I'm nervous about how different life could look. After a couple of conversations on the phone and looking over my journal entries, I think this could be the start of a dynamic summer. I *think* I am ready to see the kaleidoscope."

A big smile grew across Hu's face. He kept his eyes straight ahead instead of looking at Maria, but his smile was not hidden.

Hu had taught many students throughout the decades, but Maria's case was different. He had never heard of anyone having such specific dreams about himself and the plantation. Maria's details about the pendant, the tea house, and the precise words "wisdom and transformation" led Hu to believe there was something special about Maria's calling. He didn't know how or when, but Hu was confident that God would use Maria for something extraordinary. She just needed a mentor to point her in the right direction.

"Is there anything you need to stop to get before we leave the city?" Hu pointed out the window as he spoke.

"Just some groceries and snacks for a couple of days until I can make it back to town myself," Maria told him.

"That probably won't be necessary," he responded. "You are invited to eat meals with us. You are our guest. As for snacks, I'm sure you will find things you like in the store at the campground. We have a selection geared towards American, European, and local visitors. We even have fresh fruit and vegetables," Hu promised. "I don't think you stayed long enough to see everything we had the last time you were here."

When they arrived at the plantation, Hu drove Maria around the plantation and campground to give her a tour of the property. She hadn't realized there was over one hundred acres of tea fields, with a an impressive operation to pick, process, package and ship the tea.

Finally, Hu parked in the driveway of a small house out of sight from the campground. "This is my home," he told her. I have a particular cabin nearby where you will be staying. We will take a golf cart to get you there."

Hu pulled the golf cart up to a small secluded cabin.

"There's a WC in the cabin, but you must use the showers at the campground. I'll leave you this golf cart to get back and forth."

There was a small clearing around the cabin, and then it was surrounded by woods. On the front porch was a two-person swing. There was a fire pit in the back with three logs sitting around the fire pit as chairs. A large picnic table was just outside the back door.

Inside the cabin was a small bathroom with a commode and sink. The cottage also included a bedroom and a living room with an open kitchen area along one of the walls.

"This is wonderful," Maria exclaimed as Hu followed her inside the cabin. Admittedly, it wasn't nearly as big as her apartment back in Shanghai. But Maria loved the seclusion, surrounded by the rolling hills and forest.

"This will be yours as long as you want to stay," Hu told her. "You are welcome to stay the entire summer once we start the journey. The cabin has electricity but no hot water. That's why you need to shower at the campground pavilion. The water comes from a deep well, and is clean, drinkable water."

"This is terrific, Hu," Maria replied. "Thank you so much."

Maria placed her bags on the bed.

"There's just one more place I need to show you," Hu said. "We will walk from here."

Hu led Maria out the back door to a path in the woods. About half a mile down the trail, was another clearing.

Maria stopped, realizing this was the small one-room shack in her dream.

"Hu," Maria exclaimed, "this is the shack in my dream!"

"This is the tea house," Hu told her. "The original one was built by my ancestor, Kai. Of course, the tea house had to be replaced over the years. Also, its location was changed. The original location was roughly on the same campsite where you stayed the night you were here. But as the plantation grew and the campground was developed, the tea house needed to be moved to a private location to continue the traditions set by Kai. So while this isn't the original tea house or even the original location, this tea house is in the exact design in which Kai originally built it. The tea house is where Kai began teaching the Bible's answers to the five most essential questions of life using the Tea Room Scrolls."

Maria had to bow low to walk through the entry door. The five scrolls, wood stove, tatami mats in a traditional four-and-a-half mat layout, and the small round table surrounded by floor cushions were how Maria had dreamed it.

"If I had drawn a picture of the structure in my dream," Maria said, "this would have been what it looked like."

A big smile spread across Hu's face again.

"That's why it was so important to me that you came back," he told her. "The details you related as you described your dreams made me quite certain you had dreamt about the tea house. I don't know why you had the dreams, but God must have plans for you to be here."

Hu waited for a few seconds watching Maria's facial expressions. He wondered how she would respond to the word 'God.'

Maria was quiet for a moment. She wasn't sure about 'God.' But she decided to avoid that topic.

"What is the significance of the pendant? I bought one from your store, and I am wearing it. In my dream, you told me it represents 'wisdom and transformation.' But what does that mean?"

Hu responded with a chuckle as he headed out the door.

"We will get there," he promised. "Let's just take this slow and keep it one day, one lesson at a time. You spend the rest of the day relaxing and enjoying the peaceful environment. We will get started with the wisdom in the tea house early tomorrow morning."

Together, they walked back to Maria's cabin and made plans to meet at the tea room at 7:30 every morning. Maria was told to expect to be there for at least a few hours daily. Hu invited her to his house later that evening for dinner, something they would do every day for lunch and dinner.

In the evening, Maria drove to Hu's house for dinner. There were two other vehicles in the driveway beside the truck Hu had driven to meet Maria at the train station. He had never mentioned a wife or other family members. Maria was curious about who else could be at the house.

Maria walked up to the front porch and knocked on the door. The woman who had taken her tea order and then gave her the business card with Hu's number answered the door.

"Come in, Maria," she greeted, welcoming her in. "I'm Melissa, Hu's wife."

"Oh, hi Melissa," Maria smiled and replied. "I believe we met briefly. You gave me Hu's card and asked me to call him, right?"

Melissa was European and appeared to be several years younger than Hu. She had straight, short brown hair, cut at the shoulders, and stood around five and a half feet tall. Her smile was unmistakably kind.

"That's right. Hu and Martin are at the table. Follow me."

Hu and a young man were sitting at the table. Maria recognized him from the campground store, too. They both stood up from behind the table as soon as Maria entered the room.

"Good evening," Hu said to her. "This is my wife, Melissa, and our son, Martin. You will see them a lot in the campground and throughout the plantation.

"Hello," Maria replied. "Thanks for inviting me into your home for dinner."

Maria sat across the table from Martin, with Hu and Melissa on each end. They made small talk throughout the meal, getting to know each other.

Martin was much more attractive than Maria had first realized in the store. Besides the light skin he took from his mom, he resembled his father in every way.

Martin was courteous. He was well educated, engaged heartily in the conversation, and seemed quite intelligent. He had a friendly disposition that put her at ease. The two of them made eye contact several times during the meal. Maria's heart stirred each time.

At one point, Martin asked her directly, "Maria, tell us about your faith journey so far?"

Maria looked down at her plate, "Hmmm… until now, I have had no faith journey. Ah…I believe in being a good person?"

She looked back up at Martin and smiled.

He smiled back. "That's a great place to start, Maria."

His cheery response made her feel like she had given a good answer. But in the back of her mind, she wondered if her journey, whatever that meant, had only just begun.

After dinner, Maria promised to be back for lunch tomorrow, said her goodbyes, and walked out. Hu followed her out the door to the golf cart.

"I'll see you at 7:30 in the morning at the tea house," he reminded her.

"I'm looking forward to it," Maria replied. "Is there anything I will need to bring with me?"

"Not tomorrow," Hu answered. "I'll have a couple of gifts for you in the morning. You'll need to bring them with you going forward."

Maria turned to face the older man before getting on the golf cart to drive away.

"I want to thank you," she said. "I don't know how I would have responded if our roles had been reversed. You and your family have made me feel welcome with patience and kindness. Thank you."

Hu's infectious smile crept across his face. He reached up and tugged at his beard. "Everything happens for a reason," he quietly said. "God doesn't make mistakes, and everything happens with purpose. We'll get started in the morning. Blessings."

"Good night," Maria replied to her newly acquired friend.

He watched her drive away on the golf cart.

Maria went into the cabin and sat at a desk with her laptop. She started a new folder of journal entries. The first folder had journal entries focused on Maria's dreams. She wanted this next journal to reflect expressly on her time at the plantation.

Maria described the cabin she was staying in and the forest surrounding it. She journaled about seeing the original tea house and eating dinner with Hu and his family. Maria noted that she hoped to spend time getting to know Martin better. One of the things that grabbed her attention was how he prayed before they started eating. It was personal, thankful, and encouraging.

Praying and the Christian faith had never been a part of Maria's life. Her family attended church every year for Easter and Christmas, but that was always more of a social gathering for their family. Maria was not against the God of the Bible. She just didn't know much about Him.

Maria knew a couple of Bible stories that most children learn during childhood. She knew that Jesus was born in a manger because there was no room for Mary and Joseph at the inn. Maria knew that Jesus was killed by being crucified on a cross and that He'd performed miracles throughout His life. She also knew Christians believed Jesus had somehow risen from the dead and that He was the judge of who went to heaven and hell.

Maria was confident that she was a good person. Sure, there were some mistakes she'd made, especially the first few months she was at college away from her parents. But Maria wasn't doing anything that other kids didn't do. She didn't steal or hurt anyone else. She'd be good enough to go to heaven if heaven and hell were real. If there was a loving God who created people, He surely loved them enough that He wanted them to enjoy the life they'd been given. Maria felt that He would be ok with the life she'd lived so far.

After taking a shower and changing into her pajamas, Maria climbed into the cozy queen-sized bed. To her surprise, the bed in the cabin was much more comfortable than the one in Shanghai. It was as if she were lying on a brand new mattress explicitly made for her.

Maria was able to fall asleep within minutes of laying down.

Perfectly Proportioned

Kai sat up in bed for the first time. He was making remarkable progress in regaining strength. Healthy food and clean water were healing his body.

And the tea was deliciously unique.

Kai was in great spirits. He had just found out that Hàoyǔ had sent the man who rescued him at the river's edge. It was the second time Hàoyǔ had saved his life.

Kai was thankful to Hàoyǔ. But moreover, he was thankful to God for bringing the two of them together. Kai was sure God had knit their lives together for His purposes. He thought God must have begun something that He intended to bring Himself great glory. And Kai found solace, hope, and humility in knowing God chose him to witness His work with His own eyes. Hallelujah!

The area west of Ningde wasn't spectacularly mountainous. But it had dramatic hills. On some of these hills, a plantation had been developed.

Kai learned from the owner that the tea plantation had been in her family for four generations. It was unusual for anything to be owned by a woman in the 17th century. Yet, Leiya's (Lee-yah) family decided it was best to break tradition by leaving the plantation to their only interested child. The alternative was to crush the spirit of a woman they loved—their fiercely independent daughter.

Leiya loved the plantation. She had grown up there, worked every job, and personally perfected the wood fire drying method. It was Leiya's intelligence, dedication, and personality that had made the tea popular in the region.

So, while Leiya's passion for excellence had made the plantation successful, that trait also made her refuse every marital arrangement her parents tried. She simply said, 'No.' And allowed no discussion. She had no interest in marriage. In her experience, no man she'd ever met could let her be the woman she was. *Certainly **not** a man who would take her as a purchased possession.*

The plantation's culture of providing second chances to refugees was not Leiya's idea. Her grandfather started the tradition because he needed cheap labor and wanted to help those in need. When he was a young man, he made an error in judgment that caused him to flee his hometown. He had been adrift for a while before a stranger took him in. Decades later, when he returned to run the family plantation, he made a commitment that it would be a place of refuge.

Though it was her grandfather's idea, Leiya embraced the notion of helping people who needed second chances. She started young and had personally helped many a man and woman get settled and then thrive at the plantation. It was emotionally rewarding, and it built a loyal workforce.

So, when a man rode into the plantation with a nearly dead esteemed sea captain, Leiya decided she would oversee his recovery personally.

"How are you feeling this morning, Kai?" Leiya came into the room with a smile, hot tea, and breakfast.

"I have never been better!"

Leiya laughed. "Something makes me think you exaggerate, but I am glad you are feeling better."

He smiled up at her. And he noticed, for the first time, her striking beauty.

He had been at the plantation for two days but had slept through most of it. This morning he had been awoken by the man hired by Hàoyǔ. He told Kai who he was, who had hired him, and Hàoyǔ's instructions to him. And he told Kai that Hàoyǔ would join him here at the plantation as soon as possible.

So, Kai had awoken to improving health, grateful news about his friend and rescuer, and now realized that the angel who had been attending to him was stunningly beautiful.

Leiya was petite with a look of authority, a small package with both gun powder and compassion. Kai guessed Leiya was in her early 40's and about 5'2". She had a slim build, long black braided hair, and hands that were accustomed to hard work.

Leiya noticed Kai's attraction to her and, with body language, she immediately made it clear that she was not available.

Nonverbal communication is complex, but Kai knew it when he saw it. Kai recognized her withdrawal and took the hint. He stopped whatever he was doing that made her feel pursued. Kai wasn't interested in a relationship either; he was happy to be alive and had noticed one more thing that made him thankful.

No more noticing, Kai thought.

Kai said, "I am in a great mood because I am very grateful for everything you have done for me. And, my rescuer told me this morning about Hàoyǔ."

"Yes, I know," Leiya said smiling. "I'm happy for you, too."

As she said this, she leaned in slightly and touched his arm. Kai didn't expect this, given the "I'm not available" look he had just received.

She continued, "You both experienced extraordinary rescues! Can you tell me what happened to you after Hàoyǔ fell in the river."

Kai shared his experience of searching for Hàoyǔ, breaking his ankle, having his horse and provisions stolen, and being forced to wait with nothing but the hope of being found.

At the thought of his damaged ankle, he wiggled his foot and noticed it was not doing as well as his emotional recovery. It was painful to move, and it was bandaged.

Leiya said, "Ahh, that explains your swollen ankle. I applied some herbs and salve, and I wrapped it tightly."

She laughed and added with a scowl, "Just so you know, we all *work* here. But, you get a pass for a few days."

Leiya smiled warmly to let Kai know she was just teasing him.

"Why were you trying to come to the plantation? What are you running from, Kai?"

Kai explained that he hoped to buy some young tea plants to bring back to his family's property in northern Japan.

"Similar to here in China, tea plays an important role in Japan. The Japanese tea ceremony is paramount in business dealings, cultural events, and celebrating other connections. Furthermore, my brother wants to control the tea process to have the best ceremonial tea. Lastly, he would like to generate a profit. It will supply the Onsen with an income to keep our focus on other priorities. Do you think that you would be willing to sell me some plants?"

Leiya looked away to gather her thoughts.

She turned back to him. "Perhaps. I would need to know more about your growing conditions. But, even if the growing conditions matched, to be honest, I would need to charge a lot."

She paused and turned her gaze to the window. Rows of tea plants disappeared into the early morning fog. "It's a bigger decision, though, than growing conditions and money. Tea plants are not like fruit trees which can be more easily grown by anyone. Tea is a part of the land, part of the atmosphere, and part of the culture. The cultivar of the plant must match the cultivar of the land, which must match the cultivar of the grower. That's what makes great tea. These plants belong here."

Leiya looked over at Kai. He had a forlorn face as Leiya seemed to be telling him she wouldn't sell him any plants.

"But," she smiled, "with *that* look on your face and the fact that you've gone through such hardship to get here, yes, I will sell you a few plants."

Kai's face brightened. "Thank you, Leiya. I can promise you that your plants will be cherished. They will become a part of our heritage at Oda Onsen."

"Leiya, I have one other thing to discuss with you. I think I should let you know that my presence here could put you and the plantation in danger..."

Leiya interrupted him. "Yes, I know. I've heard this dozens of times. But somehow, it has never happened. We've had murderers, opium addicts, former members of secret societies, spies of various kinds, and many others. Something is special here. We are hard to find even with directions—you know this first hand—and the Tao seems to be always in our favor. We are doing the right thing and being rewarded for it."

"I believe you, Leiya. But the man pursuing us is convinced I possess something that threatens China. And he is determined to stop me."

Leiya tilted her head slightly in curiosity. Kai couldn't help noticing the soft curve of her neck—delicate, sweet, perfectly proportioned.

He shook his head to stop the thoughts. No more noticing, he thought.

"During the voyage from Japan, this man found out that I am a Christian. Even more than that, I have a system developed by my brother to help the Asian people study the Bible. It's a way of understanding Jesus' teachings from the Asian perspectives of Taoism, Buddhism, Shinto and Confucius thought. We were able to escape his initial attack. However, based on his threats, we have strong reason to believe he is still pursuing us."

Kai anxiously waited for a response from Leiya. There was no change to her posture or facial expression.

As the seconds drew on, Kai's heart rate picked up. She could either increase Kai's hope, be a significant roadblock, or worse, get him killed.

With no response, he continued, pouring his heart out, "Since my brother introduced me to a personal relationship with Jesus, the Son of God, my life has taken on a new meaning; I have a purpose now. My life has meaning for the first time after all these years. God created me with a plan for my life, just as He created you with a plan. After pursuing selfish desires my entire life, I have embarked on the journey for which I was created."

Kai fell silent, waiting for Leiya to say something.

Leiya looked down. Then right. Then left.

"I encourage acceptance at the plantation. Most people here have made mistakes and need a place where they can find a new beginning. I know one person here at the plantation who follows your Jesus. There could be more. They might want someone who can teach them."

Leiya paused again before continuing.

"If I could arrange something, would you be interested in meeting and teaching?" Leiya asked.

"Yes!" he responded. "This is exactly what I have been praying for. I would love an opportunity to share what I have learned with others. There is such joy to be had. I will have to wait until Hàoyǔ comes with my scrolls. They are a copy of the scrolls my brother made.

These scrolls teach the top five principles from Jesus and then how these principles apply to our daily life."

"One more thing..." Leiya started and stopped. "Ah, never mind," she said, brushing the idea out of her mind.

"What?" Kai asked. "Whatever it is, please feel free to voice your opinion."

Kai waited, hoping Leiya would continue.

She looked at Kai with a rare vulnerability in her eyes. Leiya didn't often let this emotion show. In the past, when Leiya had let her weakness show, she felt it exposed her to being over-ruled by "the man's world."

She didn't hate men. She just wanted to feel equal. She wanted to be treated as a person with worth, ideas, and opinions to consider seriously.

Every human has vulnerabilities, but when a woman expressed vulnerability in a man's world, it *proved* she was *just* a woman. She loathed being judged inferior because of her gender.

But at this moment, she felt inexplicably safe. Kai seemed different. Oddly so. He had been the captain of a ship since he was a young man. This meant he should be the quintessential man's man, the definition of power and control in a man's world. Yet, now he was landlocked, recovering from two near-death experiences, content, and nonjudgmental. He seemed open.

Moreover, he was comfortable with a willingness to risk his life for faith in something that he couldn't see or touch. This kind of zealousness was foreign to her. She believed in the Tao, but it wasn't that important to her, nor could she say it gave her the kind of happiness he seemed to have. She felt Christians were odd this way. She knew Jesus had died for something she couldn't understand, and likewise, it appeared to her that some Christians had the same peculiar resolve. Like peace within a sanctuary, they confidently loved God.

At this moment, for the first time, Leiya was seeing—or was it a feeling?—something that piqued her curiosity. Was it a sense of peace? Was it a contentment? Was it a confidence? Whatever it was, it seemed right, warm, and comforting.

She didn't know. But of one thing she was certain: the "it" she was feeling right now was not male or female. In her previous experience, everything and every situation was momentarily yin or yang.

As a child, she'd been taught that all life was a combination of opposites. The dichotomy of life was evident to her, present in everything. Even physical maladies were an imbalance of the opposites of life. Too much yin, and you needed to eat some water chestnuts to balance it. Too much yang, and you needed…

For Leiya, she had often been told that she had too much yang. According to her culture, this was why she wouldn't submit to a man in marriage.

She had believed what people said about her for a while. But as she grew older, she felt she needed to pursue a different kind of balance. She loved caring for others, looking pretty, and taking time for a walk in the wildflowers. She wanted a relationship, even marriage, but she needed to be with a *partner* who could walk alongside her as an equal, a complement, together making a difference in others' lives, and achieving something that would live on as a legacy.

She agreed that the opposites of life needed balance. The culture, philosophy, and heritage she grew up in were not wrong. She saw the same things they did. She just felt that the balance *she* needed was perhaps different than the balance her society told her was right.

Moreover, as she spent time reflecting on this through 41 years of life, she arrived at an expectation that there was a balance that could be received *spiritually*. She didn't have it, but she believed it existed. She had no basis for this assumption, couldn't describe it or explain it, and it seemed nobody in her culture agreed with her.

Unlike her culture, she believed spiritual balance was not something people could obtain on their own. According to the Tao philosophy, physical and mindful balance were worthy pursuits and momentarily obtainable. She agreed with this. But she was confident that *spiritual* balance had to be given to us spiritually and was far more critical than physical or mindful balance.

Now, sitting with Kai, she felt she was closer to this "balance giving thing." It wasn't Kai. It wasn't yin. It wasn't yang. It wasn't water chestnuts. It wasn't something to buy. It wasn't going to tell her she needed to be something else or fix her imbalance before it brought public shame to the family and community. It wasn't anything physical, chemical, emotional, or mental. It was something *spiritual*, beyond the yin and the yang, greater than the opposites.

Now, in this moment, she felt closer to discovering the "it" she knew existed. She was excited and vulnerable. And she knew she was exposing her vulnerability to a stranger, moreover, a male.

Her eyes misted as her vulnerability, curiosity, and intuition collided in response to something she had wanted for most of her adult life.

She stared at Kai, needing him to say something as the first tear rolled down her porcelain cheek. She couldn't say all that she had just thought. She could only be vulnerable in this moment. *Just* for this moment.

Kai knew something was stirring her. And he knew it wasn't him. He had been taught well by his brother and the Bible. He knew that few find the narrow gate and that he was only an instrument of God. Kai's job was simply to be willing to go where he was told and keep checking in with the Master. David had called it "Inquiring of the Lord."

His brother had told him, "God commands — Kai obeys. You got it?! Jesus said that if you love Him, you will follow His commands. And the Bible tells us that God wants none to perish. None means none, Kai. But, yet, *few* find it! Why? Maybe we just aren't good at following Jesus, going out to the highways and byways, and inviting them to the banquet. Maybe we just aren't good at reaching and teaching people where they are, in **their** culture and context, rather than imposing our culture on them. Maybe we haven't understood *and lived by* His two greatest commandments and His five greatest teachings."

In this moment, Kai knew he needed to be respectful, truthful, and relevant. Maria needed to be led, not directed. To be loved, not judged. Maybe what she needed was just a simple invitation to explore.

He finally said, "Do you think you might like to sit with the others?"

She nodded yes and left the room without another word.

Kai didn't see her for the remainder of the day.

The following day the rising sun was streaming through the window over Kai's bed. In the sunbeams, eyes barely open, he could see dust particles merrily dancing as if they were saying, "This is a great day to be alive. You are going to walk today!"

Just then, Leiya bounced energetically into his room. A waft of lavender came in with her.

Leiya had woken up feeling different this morning. Yesterday she left Kai feeling shy, open to change, and scared. She hated that feeling. Vulnerable did not fit her personality.

This morning, she was happy to be back in charge, the owner of the plantation, the one who must approve every new change. Nothing would happen at *her* plantation that didn't meet her carefully measured assessment.

But that wasn't the whole reason for her bright mood. Something else felt good this morning. Even though she had returned to her stalwart stewardship, she had woken up excited to learn about something mysterious this morning. For Leiya, mystery was playful. This morning Leiya was playful.

She wore a one-piece, black, utilitarian pantsuit. The top half of the outfit was fitted around her chest and waist, while the bottom half was loose and cut to her mid-calf. It was designed to be a practical work outfit that allowed her to move about quickly. Leiya had her hair in a traditional single braid down the middle of her back. She was feminine, efficient, and ready.

Kai watched her enter his room at lightning speed, slow herself down, and pull a chair next to his bed.

Out of respect, Kai made sure that he kept his eyes on hers. He wasn't going to overstep boundaries with any more "noticing." She was pretty, gorgeous in fact, but Kai wasn't just seeing pretty. He was seeing something else he liked. Something strong and kind, a balance of soft and firm, fun and in charge.

"It looks like you are awake with the early sun," Leiya said.

"I was just thinking the same about you. What brings you here so early?"

Leiya looked at Kai, locking her eyes on his. "I want to start to learn about your Jesus. Tonight, I want you to join me outside by the fire. Also, I think it's time for you to walk. One of my crew made some crutches for you. I'll be working most of the day, but you can tell me why Jesus is important tonight?"

Kai smiled warmly, "Today is the day, the Bible says. I'll be ready for you by the fire."

As quickly as she came, she popped back off the chair, replaced it, and swiftly left his room.

That day, as Leiya had predicted, Kai walked. Though better stated: he hobbled. With the crutches' help, he moved slowly and painfully around the house.

Kai found that his stamina was just as debilitated as his ankle. Starvation had depleted his overall strength. He walked twice that day and slept soundly after.

By nightfall, feeling accomplished and excited to talk about Jesus, he met Leiya outside.

128

There was just one wooden bench, so they sat together.

"This is my favorite time of the day, and my favorite setting." Leiya sighed and tilted her head back, looking up at the stars.

Kai relaxed back and looked up at the sky, too. His mind wandered to all the nights he sat outside with his brother Nobumasa. In front of a fire, on the side of a remote mountain in northern Honshu, his brother had instructed him long into the night.

Kai saw the world differently since falling in love with Jesus. It was no longer just a random place where people lived their lives. The entire galaxy was part of God's creation. No matter where he looked, Kai had the opportunity to experience his loving Creator. He wanted others to know this love. Kai wanted to share the love of God the Father, through His Son, Jesus, with everyone he met. As a ship captain, Kai was an expert in navigating by the stars; yet, God said that the true destination to look for in the stars was Him.

"Do the stars here look like those you see in Japan?"

Kai shared with Leiya what his brother had taught him.

"Are you saying God thinks we will find him by looking up at the stars?"

"Yes. Haven't you looked at the stars, flowers, trees, rivers, and mountains and thought: 'This couldn't possibly exist by chance. There must be a good God?'"

"Yes!" Leiya turned to Kai. "I *have* thought that. I love nature. I am inspired in nature. It's one of the reasons I wanted to perfect our tea plants and processing. I feel best when I am connected to things that grow. If I had a God, it would be the God who created all things."

Kai's eyes sparkled. "I have good news for you. The Bible says God agrees with you."

"But," Leiya had questions, "I was taught that there is not a single god."

"That is true, Leiya, according to the Bible, too. If we define god as anything supernatural, there are probably millions of gods. The spiritual world is real, vibrant, and alive. Angels minister comfort, protection, and God's will to us. There are heavenly beings who praise God day and night. And there are demons who wish to keep us from knowing and following God. Jesus even referenced twelve legions of angels who might be mustered to His aid if He called for them. According to the Bible therefore there is a multitude, perhaps even millions of gods.

"But there is also a most high God, God the Father, God the Creator. And He *has* revealed Himself to you, in the things He has made. You know this to be true, as you just said. You know the God who created all things. At least you know a little bit about Him. And the great news is that there is so much more to know — you will fall in love with Him when you get *really* close to Him."

Leiya got up and poked at the fire with an iron rod. Flames burned higher as she prodded the wood into a better position.

"But I was also taught there was no way to get *that* close to God. I was taught that the Tao changes over time. And as we try to stay in touch with the shifting Tao, we can get closer in synch, but just when we believe we are back in balance with the Tao, it is moving again."

Kai had more good news for her.

"Our educations are similar. And, I believe we were taught right. But I now believe that there is more to the story. Consider this: Jesus said *He* is the Tao, the way. Yet, to prove your point, even after three years of being with Him every day, His disciples couldn't truly understand Him as the way. One time, near the end of His earthly ministry, He told them to follow Him to where He was going and,

"You know the way to where I am going."

Thomas said to him, "Lord, we do not know where you are going. How can we know the way?"

Jesus said to him, "I am the way, and the truth, and the life. No one comes to the Father except through me. If you had known me, you would have known my Father also. From now on you do know him and have seen him."

So, the way, the Tao, is not knowable in a direct, fixed, or objectively linear sense. Instead, Jesus is knowable in the way He described to a great Jewish scholar, Nicodemus.

"Truly, truly, I say to you, unless one is born of water and the Spirit, he cannot enter the kingdom of God. That which is born of the flesh is flesh, and that which is born of the Spirit is spirit. Do not marvel that I said to you, 'You must be born again.' The wind blows where it wishes, and you hear its sound, but you do not know where it comes from or where it goes. So it is with everyone who is born of the Spirit."...."Are you the teacher of Israel and yet you do not understand these things?"

Leiya was mesmerized. *"I* want to learn these things."

Leiya stared at the fire. "But something else bothers me. I hope it's okay that I am asking many questions, but I need to understand some things."

131

She was the confident owner of the plantation again at that moment, insisting she get the correct information. Not waiting for Kai to answer, she plowed ahead.

"I meant what I said; I want to learn. But, to be honest, asking to know a God who is not *my* God is awkward."

She hesitated, and Kai could see she was searching for the right words to express her feelings. She poked at the fire a little more before she spoke again.

"It's like I have two feelings battling against each other inside of me. On the one hand, I feel oddly *compelled* to know about your God and Jesus. But, on the other hand, I feel your God is foreign. And this leads me to ask, where was your God all the time throughout China's history? Your God never showed up here. He showed up in Western Europe. Not here. And then Europeans came here and wanted to tell us about their God and that He loves us. But my first reaction is, "If He loves me, *where was He all this time?!*"

Leiya paused for a moment, mindlessly poking the fire.

Leiya finally looked up at Kai. "Do you know what that feels like?"

He could see the pleading in her eyes. And he knew her plight. She was stuck in an uncomfortable vice. On one side of the vice was a feeling of being unloved and unwanted by this foreign God, and the other side saw no logical or factual reason to continue. Both were closing in on her in a squeeze anyone would want to avoid.

Yet, when she wanted to climb out of the vice and give up *any* pursuit of God, she sensed she would be missing something vital if she didn't try to learn about God and Jesus.

"I believe I know what you are feeling. I felt it, too. Perhaps more so than you. Consider my country's history. Christianity came to Japan in 1549. Within fifty years, many came to know Jesus. My brother included. But then our country realized that Christianity was a front for imperialism, a foreign invasion intended to take away our sovereignty. My country shut down Christianity, outlawed it, and killed the Christians. My brother narrowly escaped being one of the twenty-six martyrs of Nagasaki. Today, in 1627, nearly everyone in my country believes that the Christian God is foreign. The thinking is that a God who wants to destroy Japan is not Japanese."

"So, you *do* understand." Leiya seemed relieved.

"But," she probed further, "you became a Christian anyway. Why?"

"Well, first, let me say that I didn't *become* a Christian, like someone who joins a club. Jesus doesn't call us to join a religion but to become one of His disciples. I am a disciple of Jesus Christ and only Jesus. Personally, one-on-one with Him. I don't bow to a church or organization, only to God.

"Let's also agree that people don't speak or act well for God. This is obvious; God is perfect, and we are not. Imperialists didn't represent God, only their selfish desires. We must decide to follow Christ based on Christ, not on other people's destructive behaviors. Choosing whether to follow Christ by looking at Christians is unwise. If you become a Christian, you won't be following Christians; you will be following Christ. We must look at Christ to make our decision.

"Lastly, my brother was able to educate me on my Creator and show me that my Creator God has been *with the Japanese people from the beginning*. We are the ones who forgot about Him! Our ancestors wrote about our Creator God."

133

Leiya turned full around, dropped the stick she was using to poke the fire, and sat down next to Kai.

"I don't understand. Are you saying that your ancestors wrote about the Creator God?"

"Yes," Kai turned on the bench to face Leiya. His heart skipped as he noticed her fire-lit beauty. Her soft skin glowed with a radiance of warmed brie cheese. She had let out the braid tonight, so her black hair, slightly curly from the braiding, fell gracefully across her shoulders, front, and back.

"In the Kojiki, our ancestors recorded that in the beginning were three Gods, and all three remained hidden. The first was the God of the Great and Glorious Center of Heaven, Amenominakanushi. He is the uncreated Creator — the God of the Great and Glorious Center of Heaven. It was His word that commanded Japan and the Japanese people into existence.

"The fact that He has a different name in Japan is not surprising; we speak a different language than you do. But you have a name for the uncreated Creator in your language, too. Do you know who that is?"

Leiya looked away to search her memory. "Yes, I think His name is ShangDi, The Heavenly Ruler," Leiya said.

She turned back to Kai, perplexed. "But, are you saying China's uncreated Creator is the same as Japan's?"

Kai smiled, "Well, why not? How many uncreated Creators do you think exist? It makes sense that our ancestors knew the same one, doesn't it? In Korea, His name is Hananim, God is Heaven."

Kai excitedly continued, "Think about it. How could God is Heaven, The Heavenly Ruler, and The Great and Glorious Center of Heaven be different Gods? They are all the uncreated Creator of all things. They are all unseen, benevolent, and the One who spoke everything into existence.

"On my ship, I can travel from Japan to Korea to China in just a few days. We speak different languages, but we all know the same Creator. Our ancestors all individually wrote about Him, and the records were preserved for us to know today that a benevolent uncreated Creator made everything we see around us. It seems quite logical to conclude it is the same God by slightly different names."

"Okay," Leiya responded. "I can agree the names and descriptions are quite similar."

Leiya paused.

"But," she continued. "What does this have to do with the western God and Jesus?"

"This is where it gets exciting and *proves* they are all the same." Kai smiled. "But let me back up before we go there. I want to set our language straight. Suppose we are accurate that there is no difference between Korea's Creator and Japan's Creator and China's Creator. In that case, we can surmise that every indigenous language probably has its own written history of a benevolent, uncreated Creator. Therefore, it would be somewhat inaccurate, even misleading, to speak of, for example, "China's Creator" as if it is exclusive to China. There is One who is the benevolent uncreated Creator."

"I think I see where you are going," Leiya said. "Likewise, there is no 'Western' God. Is that what you are saying?"

"Exactly."

"But…" Leiya had something to say, but the words weren't coming. In her mind, something still didn't fit. "I don't know what to say."

"How about if I try to fill in more, and maybe it will start to make sense?"

Kai knew how difficult this had been for him. His brother had given him plenty of grace in understanding this concept over many days and nights of discussion.

Leiya nodded.

"So, while most indigenous peoples wrote about the Creator, few had a culture of carefully preserving their writings. One group of people from the Middle East did. The Jews carefully transcribed from generation to generation the revelations of their ancestors.

"If we look at their writings, as preserved in the collection of forty authors written over 1500 years, we make startling discoveries. The Creator purposely caused language dispersion at one point in history. This led to people who spoke the same language congregating and migrating to various places. It isn't surprising to God, nor should it be to us, that He is known by many names.

And listen to what else He said,

> And he made from one man every nation of mankind to live on all the face of the earth, having determined allotted periods and the boundaries of their dwelling place, that they should seek God, and perhaps feel their way toward him and find him. Yet he is actually not far from each one of us, for...   what may be known about God is plain to them, because God has

made it plain to them. For since the creation of the world God's invisible qualities—his eternal power and divine nature—have been clearly seen, being understood from what has been made, so that people are without excuse.

Acts 17:26-27, Romans 1:19-20

"Does this shock you? He is close to everyone but knows He is invisible. He says He *wants* people to grope and find their way toward Him and that everyone does know of Him because they have seen evidence in all the things around them. You said yourself that if you were going to have a God it would be the one who created all things.

"Moreover, we may *feel* distant from Him, but He also says in the Bible that He loves us with an everlasting love. He says He loves us and *always* has. He yearns for us to come to Him to be a people for His own possession. Yet, can I ask you, how distant are you from ShangDi? Do you ever pray to Him? Do you seek to know Him, listen to Him, be with Him, and love Him back?

Leiya looked sheepish, "Well, no."

"Don't feel bad. I can honestly say that nearly everyone in Japan has completely forgotten about Amenuminakanushi. Our Creator is rarely prayed to in Japan. Therefore, we left Him, not the other way around.

"Leiya, I know what it feels like to be against the 'Western God.' Our country has been persecuting Christians for decades. But, when we consider what we are genuinely against, it isn't Christ or our Creator; it's imperialism. We are against being ruled by another country or culture. And we are right to be against that.

137

"But we shouldn't be against our Creator. We should get back to worshiping our Creator. In this, perhaps we could learn something from other cultures.

"Therefore, to conclude that the 'Western God' doesn't care about us because He has never been with us sounds uninformed at best. Worse yet, we could sound hypocritical. The 'Western God' is *our* Creator! And we don't even worship our Creator in our own language!"

Kai moved his foot a little on the bench and realized he was in pain. He reached down and felt his ankle. This was the first time in days that he sat without his foot propped up, so the fluids had pooled, and the swelling was painful.

Leiya didn't notice his wince. Her gaze was downward, and her mind was mesmerized and convicted by Kai's line of reasoning. More than that, she realized she was in the presence of a wise and compassionate man.

She watched him bend down, though, to touch his ankle and saw something masculine, strong, and confident in his movement. Her heart lightened in her chest. His touch... She wondered what his touch might be like on her ankle.

Kai's voice broke the spell. "I think we may have taken this conversation as far as we can tonight. I think the wind has drained from my sails."

"Of course," Leiya said, looking away, embarrassed by her thoughts.

Kai struggled to get up, but he made it fully upright. Once up, though, he got lightheaded, weak and started to sway. Leiya saw it and rushed in to steady him. To do so, she had to walk straight into his chest and hold him upright. Instinctively, he clasped his arms around her to hold on.

Locked in an embrace, Leiya's mind whirled in confusion.

It was wrong to touch like this.

It was right to help him.

It was comforting to be embraced.

It was wrong if anyone saw them, therefore, it *had* to be wrong.

It was right, though, because he was right.

It was...

Where Is My Fire?

Maria arrived 10 minutes early, but Hu was at the tea house before she got there.

"Have a seat next to that table," Hu instructed. He brought two cups and a jar of ground tea leaves from the counter. He retrieved the pot of hot water from the wood stove and prepared a cup of tea for them. There seemed to be both rhythm and routine to how he prepared everything.

The tea preparation was precisely as Maria remembered from her dream.

After everything was prepared and each item returned to its place, Hu reclined at the table across from Maria.

"In the tea room, Maria, we use a study system developed in the early 1600s by my ancestor, Oda Nobumasa. He is the son of the most famous samurai in Japanese history, Oda Nobunaga.

"Nobumasa was a hermit for nearly all his adult life, living on a remote mountain in northern Honshu, Japan. He devoted his entire life to prayer, reading the scriptures, and developing a way for the Japanese to study the Bible so they could see scripture from an Asian perspective. The background of Taoism, Buddhism, and Shinto is embedded in every Japanese citizen, including himself. Using this background, he developed The Tea Room Scrolls.

140

There are five scrolls; each scroll answers an essential question of life.

The east scroll answers the question, 'How do I grow?' People are constantly in motion; we are either growing or withering. Everyone has an instinct to grow, and therefore "How do I grow?" is a question we ponder consciously and subconsciously.

"The south scroll answers the question, 'Where is my fire?' Humans need passion in their lives, fire, adventure, and driving purpose. We all seek it in many places, yet it only exists in a dimension that few find.

"The west…"

Maria interrupted, "This is my question, Hu! This is what has been making me crazy! I came to China desperate to find something to get me away from sheer boredom. I started having dreams, got scared, pulled away, had seven days of boredom, asked again, the dreams came back, and I finally called you. *This* is my scroll, Hu. There is no need to go on."

"But, wouldn't you like me to just…"

Maria smiled. "Hu, I appreciate your diligence, but can we just start on this scroll? I am so excited that I might find some answers. **Where is my fire, Hu?!**"

Hu stood up from the table and walked over to the south scroll. "I've spent the last couple of days praying about you and the details you've shared with me about your dreams. I agree with you; this is where we must start. This, I believe, is the wisdom that is going to transform your life."

Maria squirmed in her seat like a schoolgirl. She opened a notebook and was poised to take notes.

"The south scroll represents passion, adventure, loyalty, fire, and action," Hu continued.

Hu read from the scroll. "Enter by the narrow gate. For the gate is wide and the way is easy that leads to destruction, and those who enter by it are many. For the gate is narrow and the way is hard that leads to life, and those who find it are few."

"What comes to mind when you hear these words, Maria?"

Maria reread the sentences. "I guess it reminds me of what you just said, about the other scroll, growing or withering. There are two ways to go. Two ways, hard and easy. So, I will find my passion on the hard way?"

"Good. If we notice, it is the hard way that leads to life. Life is passion. Death, or destruction, is the opposite of life and therefore, obviously, we cannot find our fire in destruction.

"What is the most rewarding activity you have ever done, Maria?"

"I was a summer camp counselor between my first and second year of college. Underprivileged kids from Berlin. They did a lot of normal summer camp stuff, but a few of us were remedial academic counselors. I taught them math through fun activities. I loved it! Unfortunately, the COVID epidemic shut it down, or I might be there right now."

"Why did you love it?"

"I was making a difference in their life. I felt good about that. I found creative ways to teach concepts that they needed to learn. And I became a friend to them, like a big sister."

"So," Hu continued, "given a choice between sitting around your mom's house playing video games all day with no other responsibilities or being the math counselor, what would you choose?"

"Of course, the math counselor."

Hu smiled. "Is one death and the other life? Is one easy and the other comparatively hard?"

Maria responded, "Yes, I see where you are going. Okay, but is this saying that I should look for the hardest way to live, and I'll find passion?"

"No, certainly not. However,...maybe...in some cases. Let's take your latest example of asking for more from life but getting scared to the point of backing off...yes, maybe we *could* say you should have stayed on the hard path."

Hu continued without pause, "But, let's not generalize in that way. Jesus is not saying that you should always seek the hardest path. This is one of His top five teachings, so something must be deeper. And there is something vastly more profound to be discovered here."

Hu stroked his beard as he formed his next words.

He pointed at the words on the scroll. "There is a narrow gate that few find. The fact that few find this narrow gate is the essence of Jesus' teaching in this scripture. The hard vs. easy way is a part of His teaching, and we just covered that. But the real depth is in the narrow gate that few find.

"If this was only about finding the hardest path to live on, every convicted criminal could claim they found the narrow gate because they chose a very bumpy, hard road."

Hu picked up his Bible and waved it. "There is something supernatural to be discovered. The Bible talks about it, though it's hard to describe. Jesus says it is like going through a narrow gate. And when you do, you will find life. That is where you will find passion, adventure, fire, and action, and you will become fiercely loyal to that gate. Few find it, but when they do, life explodes into technicolor."

Maria raised her hand. "I want this, Hu. If few find it, though, how am I going to find it?"

Hu stood up to face the South Scroll. "Do you see this little scroll within the scroll? It's tiny, but it's there. That little scroll lists the scripture we must study to find the narrow gate."

A Relationship with The Teacher

Kai's recovery continued to go well over the next several days. And Leiya's fireside chats progressed, too. During the day, she worked while Kai walked and slept. He was determined to get better, stronger, and back to full capacity.

Kai and Leiya's talks were the best part of their day. Kai looked forward to teaching about Jesus' passionate love for us. But Kai had found a new passion for himself: spending time with a woman whom he respected. She was intelligent, articulate, honest, and genuinely wanted the best for those around her. Her smile was frequent, playful, and out-shined the campfire. And she was stunningly beautiful.

For Leiya, her nightly meetings were a matter of falling in love. With both Jesus and Kai. Kai was so passionate in his descriptions of the goodness of God that it made Leiya want Jesus more. But she also knew her mind was getting made up about Kai. If he asked her to marry him, it would take but a second to yell YES. She had not revealed her heart to him, but it was already his.

One night, Kai was describing what it is like to have a regenerated spirit, to be reborn. "Now, imagine that there was a way to be more connected to our Creator. Jesus told Nicodemus that there is a way to understand spiritual things, by being born again. It is a spiritual birth in which we are re-born. There is so much to learn and explore. But the Bible says that the message of Jesus' cross will seem like foolishness until we've been spiritually transformed."

Leiya looked at Kai. Her eyes were filled with longing. "I am ready, Kai. Help me be reborn! I want this spiritual transformation!"

"I wish I could, Leiya. Being born again is something we can't do for ourselves, and nobody else can help us either."

"But I am ready, Kai." Leiya tilted her head in an innocent pleading.

Kai reached out to take Leiya's hand. It was an instinct with no intimacy meant to be conveyed.

Before he reached her hand, he suddenly realized this could be taken the wrong way. He caught his breath, but he kept going, knowing he was taking a risk that she might feel it crossed her boundary.

Leiya responded instinctually, too. She let Kai take her hand and warmly responded by bringing her other hand over.

Kai said, "I wish I could give you better news. Unfortunately, Leiya, even if we feel we are ready, we can't decide; only Jesus decides who is ready.

"But the good news is that the more we pursue Jesus, the sooner He will deem us ready for spiritual transformation. Right now, in this very moment, *you are pursuing Jesus* and growing closer to Him. It feels right, doesn't it?"

Kai glanced down at their embraced hands, unintentionally giving a double meaning to "it feels right."

Leiya withdrew her hands with a demure glance at Kai. "It does," she said.

Leiya blushed. It did feel right. All of it. She knew in her heart that she was going to find God. But Kai felt right, too. She wanted a lifetime of that intimacy.

His hand was like a key unlocking a mysterious, neglected box that had been shoved under her bed since she was twelve. That summer, she had a crush on a young man who had come to the plantation with his mom. They left within a week, never to return. Leiya's heart had grown a lifetime in that week. When he left, tears were not allowed. She closed the box and tucked it away from sight so it wouldn't tantalize her. Romantic love had been found, lost, and locked away.

It might have stayed shut and hidden for the rest of her life. Leiya was confident that she had thrown the key away forever and nobody would find it.

But, a couple of weeks ago, a man had ridden through the gates to the plantation, nearly dead, roped onto the back of his horse. And with each passing day, as he revived and re-gained life, she was finding a new life, too.

She shook her shoulders to rid herself of the embarrassing thoughts. She regained her composure and returned to the substance of their conversation.

"But you came here to teach, Kai. If we can't learn anything that is going to help us be reborn, why should we be taught?"

Kai smiled. "Yes. Some pursue knowledge. Others want to learn and apply the knowledge. Still others, though, commit to a relationship with the teacher Himself. It's those last disciples to whom Jesus will choose to reveal the Father through rebirth.

"So, yes, I have come to teach, but I don't know who will want just to learn, who will want to learn and live by the teachings, and those who decide to let themselves fall in love with Jesus. The last group is the true disciples of Jesus, who will likely be born again. This is where religion and rules melt away and where the joy begins. Do you want to fall in love?"

Kai looked at Leiya with innocent eyes.

Leiya smiled at the question. She knew he was asking about falling in love with Jesus. But she was falling in love with two men simultaneously. A man who died to give her access to God, and a man who nearly died to tell her about the first One.

She answered honestly, "Yes, I know I am falling in love. Indeed, I believe I am truly in love."

Leiya turned away and choked on her emotion. Private thoughts are like little messages we play for ourselves in our heads. Nobody gets into our thoughts; they are ours. But when we speak those thoughts, suddenly, we've exposed our inner sanctuary to ridicule and loss.

But the micro-second of fear was immediately followed by solace and relief that the words were out now. Leiya had publicly admitted she was in love. And she knew this love was for Jesus. The emotion she felt, the raw reaction, was to express her love for Jesus.

She felt something quicken in her heart, a spark, a release, a lightening of burden, a love of epic proportion filling her up, choking out any more words. She had no more words. They were drowned beneath the filling.

She lifted her eyes to heaven, wanting, needing, aching to express her thanks to her Creator. She was overwhelmed with love. The filling that had overtaken her was pure, white, beautiful, enthralling love. Her need to express gratitude gurgled up through the filling and burst through as non-sensical words. Like a song of love, she uttered sounds of pure joy. The meaning of each word was unknown to her, but it didn't matter. She knew the overall sense, a love song to her Savior, Jesus Christ.

Kai waited and prayed in thanksgiving while she sang to her new Lord. Not every person's experience is the same, but Kai was quite sure what had happened. She had let in the God who created the heavens and all we see. She let in the Spirit of Christ to fill her with abundant life and the fullness of joy He promised to those who love Him. Leiya had just walked through the narrow gate.

Over the following weeks, Kai's ankle healed nearly wholly, and Leiya found several plantation workers interested in learning the Bible. Kai realized that God was gathering a flock to teach, so the tearoom teachings needed to start.

Kai found a remote site for the tea house, and he and two other plantation workers built the house out of bamboo. It wasn't built to last long, but the roof didn't leak, and it could hold twenty or so students. Kai was pleased; it was sufficient for the near term. Furthermore, it doubled as a home for Kai.

Without the scrolls, Kai planned to teach from memory. He knew the top five teachings and some of the grid. He trusted that God would supply the scriptures and education as the class progressed.

Kai had taught several lessons when they finally received word from the blacksmith that Hàoyǔ was ready to travel. Kai rejoiced and went the next day to pick him up.

When Kai arrived, Hàoyǔ was awake and ready to travel. Their reunion was tearful. Kai owed Hàoyǔ his life twice, and as he hugged and thanked him for saving his life, he couldn't entirely choke back the tears. Sea captains don't cry, but this one did, as he realized that not only had Hàoyǔ saved his life, but God had spared him to live for His will, His work. The responsibility and blessing were on his shoulders. There was work to do at the plantation, and Kai was excited to get the scrolls back and add Hàoyǔ to the tearoom class.

Hàoyǔ still could not walk without a significant amount of pain, nor was he able to ride a horse. So, the blacksmith had built a small trailer for Kai to pull behind his horse.

The following day back at the plantation, Kai arose with a purpose. He retrieved the five scrolls and laid them out on the floor. The scrolls gave the top five teachings of Jesus Christ. He'd already generally talked about the scrolls' Bible study method. But now, he needed to go into more depth.

Kai closed his eyes and thought to himself for a few moments. He remembered how his brother first started teaching him. They had started with the east scroll. The east scroll spoke of growth and new beginnings. Each of the five scrolls contained God's answer to one of humanity's most essential questions. The east scroll answered our question, "How do I grow?"

Nobumasa had said that humanity was never intended to live in stagnation. Stagnation, he surmised, was headed towards death while growth moves us toward life. We aren't comfortable simply existing. We need more than that. We need purpose in our lives. We need to know we are growing, learning, expanding, producing new fruit, and giving in new ways.

Nobumasa believed that God agreed with that viewpoint, and he found a significant body of scripture that proved God Himself was directing us to move in the direction of life. God wants us to find life in more abundance, drink of the living water, rather than wallow in tepid still water, festering with disease, sin, and death.

Kai decided to teach the east scroll first.

That first evening after he had the scrolls hung, he pointed to the east scroll and said, "Who among you believes there is more to life than what you are doing today?"

All ten students raised their hands.

"Have you ever wondered *if* there is more? Does your mind yearn to *learn* more? Does your heart yearn to *love* more? Does your spirit yearn to *know your Creator more*?"

All ten students continued to raise their hands.

"Have you ever asked the essential question, **HOW** DO I GROW? How do I grow as a man or woman, as a spiritual being, as someone who is groping to find the God who has the power to be *my* refuge, the God who is on *my* side, and has the power to help *me* grow for the remainder of *my* life?"

The students held their hands up until Kai said, "If you are serious, God has told us how we are to grow. We will study all of the scriptures leading up to this teaching but realize the top of the scrolls is the pinnacle teaching. This is one of the top five teachings of Jesus

151

Christ. It's a big one, like an enormous firecracker. It's okay if you don't get it immediately; you will in time.

"Late one night a powerful, learned Jewish man came to Jesus looking for some answers. He didn't understand who Jesus was, but he knew Jesus was sent from God based on the various miracles Jesus had performed. Nicodemus was a top Bible scholar; if anyone had understood who Jesus was, he would have. But He didn't, so he came inquiring. Paraphrased, his inquiry was, "How could this be, and how does this relate to my own life?"

Kai pointed at the scroll again and said, "Here, on this scroll is the answer Jesus spoke."

> Jesus answered, "Truly, truly, I say to you, unless one is born of water and the Spirit, he cannot enter the kingdom of God. That which is born of the flesh is flesh, and that which is born of the Spirit is spirit. Do not marvel that I said to you, 'You must be born again.' The wind blows where it wishes, and you hear its sound, but you do not know where it comes from or where it goes. So it is with everyone who is born of the Spirit." John 3:3-8

That night, after the students went to their bunks, Leiya stayed behind to spend some time with Kai. Their relationship had progressed. They kept the relationship biblical but made no pretense in front of everyone. They were both clearly in love with each other.

Tonight, Kai was unusually quiet while he lit the fire.

Leiya waited until the fire was going and then stood directly behind Kai. She wrapped her arms around his waist and gently kissed the back of his shoulders.

She whispered, "Is something troubling you this evening?"

Kai turned around and faced Leiya. He looked down into her eyes and deeply sighed. Kai pulled Leiya's arms away from his waist and held her by both hands. Kai's eyes were strained with the weight of a problem he was contemplating.

"My 40 days is about up, Leiya," he said. "My crew and ship will arrive at the port in Shanghai in six days."

Kai let go of her hands and took a few steps away, staring off into the distance in the other direction.

"The man who was pursuing Hàoyǔ and I know what the plans were. He knows when I was supposed to meet the ship. He and his men will be waiting for me to arrive. I don't know how I will get around them to my ship. And I don't even know what to tell them when I get there."

"Don't go," Leiya interrupted. "Stay here and start a new life with me. You are needed here. There will always be new workers arriving at the plantation. There will always be new people to introduce to Jesus and teach the Gospel. You are needed here. The Christian community you started would be lost without you," she pleaded.

She walked over to him and touched his hair. "And so will I."

"I want to stay too. Leiya, I am in love with you. But…"

Kai paused for a minute, allowing Leiya to hear the seriousness in his voice.

"I can't abandon my crew. They will wait for me and be in danger they know nothing about. I've thought about it, and I need to direct them to the port in Ningde. If I can get them to change ports, I can load them up with some tea plants and send them back to Nobumasa. Plus, Nobumasa will be thrilled to know that Asians here are turning to Jesus."

Leiya knew Kai was right. He was a man of both loyalty and integrity. He would not leave friends and loved ones wondering if he were dead or alive.

She said, "What if we send someone else to the ship?"

"I thought about that, but I can't ask anyone to do that for me."

"I can," Leiya said. "Someone will volunteer."

Wei, one of the students, readily volunteered. He wasn't from Shanghai, but he was familiar with the port. Kai and Leiya decided that the less Wei knew about why he was going instead of Kai, the safer it would be for him. Kai told him what to look for to identify the ship and let him know that Enji would be the man in charge. Wei was given a specific message to say and a written letter from Kai to Enji, explaining the situation in brief detail of why he needed to sail the ship to Ningde. On the night before Wei set out for Shanghai, the Christian community prayed over Wei for a safe journey.

A week later, Leiya led Kai outside the building, pulling him by the hand. She was excited, giddy, like a teenage girl. Kai liked seeing this side of her.

Kai finally made it out of the building, and Wei, Enji, and two other men from the ship's crew stood there.

"Enji!" Kai exclaimed, embracing his closest friend. "How was the sailing from Japan?"

Enji gave a cheerful laugh, returning his captain's embrace. "It was smooth sailing until we reached Shanghai. Things became confusing once we arrived, but we finally made it to you."

Kai welcomed his three friends to the plantation and then warmly embraced Wei. "I will always be indebted to you," Kai said, looking Wei square in the eyes.

"Where's the rest of the crew?"

"They remained on the ship," Enji responded. "I imagine they will take turns roaming Ningde. In all honesty, it was a rough voyage. The weather was difficult for the first three days after setting sail. I'm sure they will enjoy a night in the village along with the ship's comforts for rest."

"Enji, allow me to formally introduce you to Leiya. She has become *very* important in my life and will remain so."

Kai took Leiya by the hand and pulled her closer to him.

Enji looked at Kai, then to her, then to their clasped hands, and back to Kai.

"Ahh, I see."

He then turned to face Leiya directly and addressed her.

"Well, in that case, you have just become very important to me, Leiya."

Enji bowed before her and smiled. "I am at your service, Leiya. You can count on me. Truly, you can count on me to protect, defend, and provide for you."

Leiya bowed back.

"I am humbled. It's nice to meet you finally," Leiya said to Enji. "Kai has told me a lot about you and your travels together."

Hàoyǔ hobbled over just then, and Kai introduced him as the man who had saved his life twice. Once again, Enji deferentially paid respect to him and thanked him for keeping his captain alive.

After dinner, Kai, Leiya, Enji, and Hàoyǔ sat around the fire, sharing stories about Kai and Enji's travels and the history of the plantation.

Leiya finally asked the big question on her mind. She knew Kai planned to travel back to Japan with the plants. Looking at Kai and Enji, she asked, "When will you be leaving?"

The group went quiet. Sitting as close as he could to Leiya, Kai turned his head and focused on Enji. "What are you thinking?" Kai asked his friend.

Enji sat up straight on his stump and cleared his throat. "A few members of the crew need to get back to Japan as quickly as possible. Taking the time to sail here from Shanghai has set us back a little. We need to set sail no later than early tomorrow afternoon."

"I will make arrangements for some of the workers to transport and load 10 mature tea plants in the morning then," Leiya said subtly.

Later that night, Leiya asked Kai privately, "You have to leave, don't you?"

"It's not forever," Kai responded.

"How soon will you be back," Leiya asked almost in a whisper, afraid of Kai's answer.

"I'll be back in three weeks, at the longest," Kai answered. "Probably closer to 14 days than 21."

Leiya stopped, took Kia by both hands, and plumbed the depths of his sweet eyes.

"After you had been here for a while, part of me was hoping that you were making up a story about having to take tea plants back to Japan and that you would always be here."

Leiya briefly paused, trying to come up with the words she wanted to say.

"I need you, Kai," Leiya said. "This plantation needs you. We need you to be the one here, sharing the Gospel with new believers. But, more than that, my heart needs you. Promise me that you will be back?"

"I promise, Leiya," Kai answered her.

Kai paused for a few moments.

"I'm falling in love with you, Leiya. You are everything a man could want. Intelligent, articulate, giving, honest, and beautiful. Even more than that, I believe God put you in my life for a specific reason. Not because I was in danger and needed a place to hide, but because I'm supposed to spend the rest of my life with you."

Kai let go of Leiya's hands and wrapped his arms around her. He looked down at her face. "I am coming back, Leiya. I promise. I will return to you within the next three weeks."

Leiya rested her head on Kai's chest, savoring every word he said to her. She believed what he was saying. The thought of spending forever with him brought peace and comfort to Leiya. Kai was the man she didn't think existed; she had given up on men. But God had another plan for her. He sent her Kai to discover that love was obtainable from a man *and* Him.

Kai held her close, stroking the back of her head. "I want to ask you something, my sweetness," Kai said.

Leiya gently took her head off his chest and looked up at him. She scanned his eyes as he searched his heart for his next words.

He saw devotion in her eyes. He knew she was fully committed to him. His eyes misted from the emotion of knowing she was the only one. At forty-five years old, only twice had he given himself entirely. The first time was to the sea—the second time to Jesus.

"I guess what I am wondering is… I want to spend the rest of my life with you. When I return from Japan, will you be my wife, Leiya?"

Have You Ever Been in Love?

Hey there," Martin said as she walked through the screen door. "How's your afternoon been?" he asked.

"Good," Maria responded as she walked to the counter. "I spent some time reviewing what your dad taught me this morning."

"That's good," he smiled. "The old man will make you think if you listen to him long enough."

Maria laughed. "I think that's one of the things I like the most about him," she answered. "That's why I wanted to talk to you."

"What's on your mind?" he questioned.

"I appreciate your dad, but I wondered if Jesus is as important to you as He is to your dad?"

Martin stopped what he was doing behind the counter and gave Maria his full attention. It reminded her of the way Hu talked to her.

"My faith in Jesus Christ is the most important part of who I am," Martin responded while looking Maria square in the eyes. "Without Him, I'm nothing. I don't even want to think about what life would be without Jesus being the center of it."

"How do you do that?" Maria questioned.

159

"Do what?" he replied.

"Live life with that mentality," Maria continued. "With school, friends, planning your future and enjoying this part of your life. How do you fit Jesus into all that?"

"Jesus isn't a part of my schedule," Martin told her. "He is the paper on which my schedule is written. Enjoying life as He intended is impossible unless He is the King."

Maria placed her elbows on the counter and rested her head in her hands. She wanted the confidence in God that Martin just spoke. Maria had never believed in anything this way. He spoke confidently about God; a trust Maria rarely witnessed in anyone. Moreover, she found his love for Jesus attractive. It made Maria want to know both Jesus *and* Martin a lot better.

"Have you always felt so strongly about Jesus?" Maria continued.

"No," Martin told her. "My faith is something my mom and dad always encouraged. But, just growing up with encouragement is only the start. At a young age, I started placing trust in God, and when you find that obedience to God has rewards, you want it more. The fun is in *partnering* with the God of the universe. There is no better way to live. I said fun, and I mean it. I simply believe God, which makes me want to watch Him work, and then when I see Him do things, I am giddy."

Martin recognized the look on Maria's face. He had seen the same look on many people who weren't raised the way he was. It was a mixture of "I don't get it," and "That does sound kind of cool."

"Okay, but as someone my age, what suggestions do you have for me?"

Martin gave a laugh. He cranked his neck backwards and said, "Well, *before* I can answer *that* question, how old *are* you?"

Maria smiled, too. "I'm 21 and just finished my third year of college."

"I'll be 21 in two weeks."

Maria continued to smile. She liked him. "I'll have to remember that, soon-to-be-birthday boy!"

"Well, let's see if I have any advice. Probably the best advice I have is to get to know Jesus' top five teachings. It's the top scripture on each of the five scrolls. Studying those tearoom scrolls will teach you what you *must know*. It's a great place to start because Jesus has answered the five most important questions everyone has on their minds. So, start with some facts about His teachings.

"But beyond knowledge," he continued, "as one young adult to another, I would recommend that you don't set out to become a 'perfect' Christian. There is no such thing. Transformation takes time. If you have spent 21 years walking into the woods, you should expect it to take a little time to make your way out."

Martin grabbed a broom and started sweeping around the counter in the shop. "Next, my observation is that most people, even those who attend church, don't really know what Christianity is. Jesus doesn't want someone just to believe; He wants us to love Him. To fall in love with Him. Have you ever been in love?"

Martin stopped sweeping as he asked the question. It was a serious question, and he wanted to emphasize the question by looking at her.

He looked at her face, down her frame to her feet, and back to her face.

He suddenly flushed with embarrassment as he realized he appeared to be physically checking her out, unintentionally being provocative. He turned around and went back to sweeping, hoping he hadn't offended her. But he also couldn't help thinking about what he saw; she was gorgeous.

This would have frustrated Maria back home in Germany. She was not an object to be ogled. Yet, here, thousands of miles from home, Maria was surprisingly calm in the presence of an attractive, kind, and intelligent man.

She ignored the look and said, "No, I can't say I have."

"If you stick around the tea room, Maria, it will happen soon."

Just then, they were interrupted by the sound of the shop's screen door opening. It was Martin's replacement. His shift was over, and it was time for him to go home.

As they left the store together, Martin turned to Maria, "There's something else I'd like to tell you. Should we ride together back to my house? Besides, it's almost dinner time. Are you okay with spending a little more time together?"

Maria felt a lightening in her heart at "time together." That sounded nice.

They got on the golf cart. She instinctively got in the passenger side, and he got in the driver's side. She turned slightly sideways to be able to look at him as he drove. He started to tell her something, but although she wanted to hear, she couldn't. Her mind was screaming

162

at her. "I could get used to this. I like this guy! He's handsome. I mean, look at him. And he is talking about God and has no idea I can't hear him. I want to reach over and touch his cheek. I should have asked him if he was ever in love with anyone. I wonder what he would do if I did both?"

She suddenly reached over and, realizing the cheek was too bold, she touched his shoulder with the back of her hand. "I'm sorry to interrupt, but I just realized I told you I was never in love with anyone. What about you?"

Martin flushed. It occurred to him that she probably hadn't heard a word he said about his favorite passage, James 4:8.

"Ahh...well...besides God. To be honest, I don't think so."

He flipped open his hands on the wheel and added, "Why did you ask that right now?"

It was Maria's turn to be embarrassed. She had never acted on such impulse. It was unlike her, and she wished she could take it back. But, the urge continued.

"Oh, I don't know, I just wondered. How about infatuation? I can honestly say I was fascinated with a guy in Calculus class, but he wasn't interested, and we never even dated. Surely there were some women you were interested in?"

Martin kept his eyes on the road. He didn't know what to say. In his mind's eye, he saw her beauty and felt her hand on his shoulder. Infatuation? If he were honest, at this moment, the answer would be, "Yes, with you." But he wanted to avoid those words. This was just a woman who needed to find God. He prayed, God, help me; I'm in over my head right now. Is she someone you want me with in anything more than just helping her learn about you? In his spirit, he felt a 'Yes, more.'

Martin pulled off under a tree to be in the shade. He turned to Maria. He looked into her eyes and saw sweetness and innocence.

Martin spoke. "I want to be honest with you, Maria. You asked me about infatuation. I am feeling infatuation with *you*, Maria. Truly, I don't know what to do about that. I believe you are here to learn about Jesus, not for a relationship with anyone else but Him. But, I am attracted to you, and my heart has reacted to you every time I see you. And when you just touched me, my whole insides responded viscerally; something deep inside me felt like I was experiencing comfort and goodness. I hope I am not making you feel uncomfortable."

As he said that last sentence, he knew he wasn't making her feel uncomfortable. Instead, she was like a Boston cream pie melting against a warm fork. She was ready, in a mixture of demure and relief, glad he had said what she couldn't.

She had no words. She didn't know what to do either. He had to decide. She felt that it was in his hands.

He saw the pleading silence in her eyes.

"I think the best thing is to keep going as we were. You need to fall in love with Jesus, not me. So, let's keep going. If God wants us to be together in any other way, He'll make it clear. In the meantime, I will not ignore my feelings for you. They are real, but I am confident that God will lead us."

He reached over and offered his hand to her, palm up. "Are you okay with this? Letting God lead us?"

She immediately put her hand in his. Still looking directly in his eyes, she nodded her head. "Uh-huh, I am."

Then, she drew his hand closer to her before she let it go. It was her way of affirming that she was *good* with everything he had said.

While waiting for dinner, Martin got another chance at the house to tell Maria about James 4:8.

"Don't you love this! God tells us that He will draw near to us if we draw near to Him. I love this promise. It's God at His most obvious best. He won't force us to love Him. Moreover, He waits for us to take the first moves. But if we want a relationship with Him and take steps to get close, He promises to be there *and* respond by drawing near to us."

It was another delicious dinner filled with morsels of Melissa's cooking and God's Word. Near the end, Martin invited Maria to join him on a trip to Ningde the next day.

Seasoned By Fire

Sea travel is dangerous. During Kai's thirty years at sea, there were times he wanted to kiss the ground when he finally reached the shore.

But never was he this excited to get off a ship. It had been 16 days since he left Leiya to return to Japan with the tea plants. They were some of the longest days of his life.

It was late morning when Kai, Hàoyǔ, and Enji made it to the plantation. Leiya noticed Kai approaching from a distance long before he saw her. She dropped the basket she was carrying and ran to Kai as fast as possible. When Leiya finally reached Kai, she melted into his arms and softly sobbed.

"I've missed you so much," she whispered.

"Oh, my love, I have missed you. My heart was sick without you. I am excited to make you my wife—it's what I have thought about for 16 days. Thank you, Lord, for bringing me back safely."

"Hallelujah and amen," Leiya added. "I have been praying and reading the Bible every day, Kai. I am feeling so close to Him lately. But, come, let's get everyone inside."

Leiya invited the three of them into her home and fed them lunch. Leiya surprised Kai by saying the prayer before the meal.

"Heavenly Father," she began. "Thank you for allowing Kai and his crew to return to Ningde safely. Thank you for the desire you have given us to grow closer to You in everything we do. We desire you to use this plantation however you see fit, Lord. We surrender everything we are to you, your Word, and your will. We love you and ask for this in Jesus' name, amen."

Kai noticed the power and devotion Leiya expressed through the prayer. He had left her some material to read and study when he'd gone to take the tea plants back to Japan. Leiya had grown closer to Jesus since Kai's departure. Kai's heart was soaring.

Lunch included entertaining stories as Enji shared some funny and embarrassing tales at sea with Kai. Leiya kept asking for more; it was fun to learn about her fiancé, and it touched her heart to see the close bond between the two men.

Enji said, "Leiya, I want to thank you for the meal, but I must return to the ship soon. We have cargo on board the ship that needs to go to Korea and some goods we will be picking up there. We need to leave before dusk."

Kai added, "Before I forget, my brother was hoping you could send ten more plants to him?"

"Yes, I'll have a few workers load up the plants. Then, what if we accompany Enji back to the ship, Kai? I'd love a tour."

They arrived with the plants by late afternoon. Kai brought Leiya aboard. It was the first time she'd been on a ship.

When they got to the Captain's quarters, she asked, "Are you going to miss this?"

167

He nodded as he looked around. "Yes, but I believe God is calling me elsewhere. It seems He has changed my trajectory. I discussed this with my brother when we were at the Onsen; he said this is how God works. Nobumasa said that God lets us steer most of the time, but when He needs us to change course, He'll take the rudder *and* give us peace about the change. He has given me peace."

A breeze blew through the open window, a wind of change that made them both shiver.

Once everything was loaded, Enji and a few members of the ship's crew exited the ship with Kai, Leiya, and Hàoyǔ. There were a few supplies to procure before embarking.

As they rounded a corner, suddenly, Hàoyǔ stopped and grabbed Kai by the shirt.

"Oh no," Hàoyǔ whispered just loud enough for Kai and Enji to hear him. "It's Yìchén."

Yìchén spotted Kai and Hàoyǔ right away. He had three other men with him. The four of them approached.

Kai's first thought was to protect Leiya. In his first conversation with Leiya, he had warned her about the danger of keeping him at the plantation, but she had brushed it off. Now, as he feared, that danger was right in front of them.

Kai instinctively stepped in front of Leiya as Yìchén, and his men walked closer. Enji gave a loud whistle to get the attention of the other men waiting on the ship.

"I told you never to stop running, and yet, here you are," Yìchén said. "Did you think you would escape from my home and never see me again?"

"And you," Yìchén said, taking a few steps towards Hàoyǔ until he stood directly in front of him. "Did you believe you could stay in Asia and never cross my path again?"

Enji shuffled closer to Yìchén. "Hey, my friend, you were desperate to find a way back to Shanghai. Kai graciously allowed you to take a role on our ship so you could make it home. He didn't need to do that for you. You should have spent the rest of your life thankful to this man. Instead, you want to threaten his life in front of me?"

They heard running boots. Yìchén looked past Kai and saw many of Kai's crew approaching fast. He stepped back in front of Kai, whispering where no one else could make out what was being said.

"You might have been able to escape this time because your crew is here to protect you. But, next time, you won't be as lucky. Let me catch you by yourself and see what happens. Then we will see how much Jesus can protect you."

Yìchén and his men backed away with their eyes on Kai. Then, he started loudly laughing as the men from Kai's ship finally were in range to hear.

"No need to be all uptight," Yìchén told them. "We were just on our way. We'll meet again," he said, looking at Kai. "I'll see you real soon, captain."

Enji turned to Kai. "Say the word, Captain, and we'll end this right now."

"Let them go. We would make a scene where many people know Leiya. Yìchén has no idea who she is or where to find us. Let's just get on our way."

"Can I make a suggestion?" Enji asked. "Let's get everyone on board and stay until dark. Then, a few of us will be able to get you back to the plantation. It will be much safer under cover of darkness."

It was many hours later when they arrived back at the plantation. They had not only waited for darkness but also made a circuitous path to the plantation to avoid being followed.

"Home sweet home," Leiya said as they passed through the gates.

Just then, they heard screaming and a loud rushing and crackling.

The two of them ran up the hill. At the top of the hill, they saw people running around Leiya's house frantically.

Smoke was billowing out the windows, and flames engulfed most of the roof. Within seconds, Leiya's childhood home was utterly consumed in fire.

Leiya fell to her knees. Kai knew it was too late to save the home. Rather than running to watch it burn, he bent over Leiya and hugged her.

Kai had always been good with words. But he knew words would not take away the sorrow Leiya was feeling. Her home had been in her family for generations. It was where Leiya's family had lived since her great, great grandfather. Her mom had left her the home and plantation when she passed away just over ten years ago.

They sat together on the hill, Kai holding her close, watching the fire from a distance.

Kai said, "Leiya do you remember when we were studying the South Scroll, and we discussed that our passion, action, adventure, and loyalty come from entering the narrow gate, but that the gate was on a *hard* path?"

She nodded.

"The last scripture on that scroll teaches us how to trust in God's grace when the path is hardest. The scripture on Point 8 South Scroll says we are just a jar of easily broken clay, so that we remember God is the One with all surpassing power. Jesus describes how to live in His flow of joyous blessings; these are Points 1-8 on the scrolls. But his most startling teaching is in Point 8, Jesus' last beatitude; we are blessed with the Kingdom of Heaven *when we are persecuted for righteousness' sake.*

"This scripture is for times like this when we are, like your tea, becoming seasoned by fire. Most Christians will never be tested like this. But if we are tested by persecution, even broken, the scripture shows us that we are hard pressed on every side, but not crushed; perplexed, but not in despair; persecuted, but not abandoned; struck down, but not destroyed.

"My love," Kai stroke Leiya's cheek, gently wiping tears, "we can trust that God is flowing His grace into us right now, in the heat of the fire. And that when the fire is over, He will work this to our good and His good."

Leiya looked up through flowing tears and said, "I believe. I'm really sad, but I believe."

When they went down to the fire, Hàoyǔ told them, "Someone saw three men riding off the plantation on horses towards Ningde moments after the house went up in flames. I'm positive this was Yìchén. He's done this more than once to get a message across. He saw Leiya with us at the port. Someone in town must have told him how to find her."

Leiya stayed with Kai at the tea house that night. She read the Bible verses Kai had referenced earlier and was at peace. She fell asleep quickly.

As she slept, Kai prayed for Leiya. That God would pour even more grace out to her. When anyone else would have been crushed under the circumstances, Leiya had found a peace that night. God had already brought His Word to her amidst real-life persecution, and she had found the grace of God. Kai also asked God to bless them as a married couple with a long life living in the Kingdom.

Kai slept peacefully, too.

The next day Leiya woke up excited. Kai was still dozing when she woke him.

"Kai, we must talk. God spoke to me last night. It happened in my dream. It had to have been Him. I just know it. There's no other way it could have happened."

Kai propped up on his elbows, clearing his sleep-filled head.

"God wants both of us here, at the plantation. We need to build another house. My family's past was important to me but *now* is when the real future begins. This is our family's future, yours and mine. Our family will revolve around Jesus and sharing the Gospel with others. That's where you and the scrolls come in."

"Keep going, my love" Kai said after Leiya had stopped for a few moments.

"Kai," Leiya continued, "this plantation will always be *your* home. Our descendants will live here for generations. But you are going to be gone a lot. God said that you are the person He has chosen to share the Gospel throughout Asia, teaching the Tea Room Scrolls method of studying the Bible everywhere you go."

The excitement left Leiya's face. Her voice lowered. "There is more, though."

Kai reached over to take her hand.

"Last night's persecution was the beginning," Leiya told him. "God told me things will happen that neither of us understands. But, *regardless* of what happens, *you* must stay faithful to what God has called you to do. Christianity in Asia depends on your willingness to stay faithful to leading others to Jesus."

Both Leiya and Kai were quiet for a few moments.

Kai finally said. "So, this sounds a bit ominous. Was there more? What is it that's going to happen that might throw me off the mission?"

Leiya cleared her throat before talking. "It's not your fame and prosperity that will lead others to Jesus, Kai," she continued.

"People will not follow Jesus because of how great your life is, or who your father was. Instead, my dream showed me that you will experience things that would crush any other man. Regardless of what you go through, no matter how hot the fire gets around you,

you must press on in Christ. He will test you with fire *and* bring you through. Many times."

"Your pain, suffering, and willingness to keep pushing on for the sake of the Gospel, much like Paul, will be a sign for others that you are truly carrying God's truth in Asia."

Kai looked up at the ceiling. He had prayed last night. Was this the answer to that prayer?

"I don't know," he finally said. "Are you sure this was a dream from God? It could be a nightmare from the enemy. I mean, I do not doubt you, just thinking out loud. We are told to test the spirits. Not to believe everything, but to search the scriptures to ensure it is in line with God's Word."

Kai stroked his long beard for a moment. "But, now that I am thinking aloud, what you say *is* in line with God's Word. As you mentioned, Paul endured multiple near-death experiences, beatings, imprisonments, stonings, and lack of food and shelter. All for the Gospel. And He was *joyful* all the while!"

"There is one more thing," Leiya added softly. "I believe God will prove the dream true. He told me to go back to my house. There's something we will find in the debris of the house, something that will be a part of all of this."

"What is it?" Kai asked.

"I don't know. But I believe we will know it when we find it. The last thing He told me was the *purpose* of the thing we find. It will be a sign to future generations of our family, the Oda clan, and remind us why we must keep going, even when we are stumbling, carrying our

174

cross, all the way back to Japan. It is not a thing to be worshipped, just a sign of God's enduring love for Japan."

"Japan?"

"I don't know, Kai. I am just repeating what God told me."

"Okay," Kai said. "Let's go to your house and look around. We place our trust in Him."

The debris was still smoldering in places, making it difficult to handle without the risk of burning themselves. They searched the periphery for a while, but nothing was catching their attention.

They decided they needed to come back the next day. Leiya went to work, and Kai returned to the tea house to prepare for the next lesson.

Kai's eyes shot open. He had dozed off momentarily and saw the object in that light-headed dream-like state between sleep and awake. He jumped to his feet and darted out of the tea house door. Several workers stopped what they were doing as they watched Kai sprint across the plantation.

Leiya, Hàoyǔ, and a group of other workers were discussing tea shipments in front of a building. She spun around to watch as Kai sprinted to the burned debris. Leiya couldn't resist, and ran back to the house.

Kai stepped confidently through the smoldering embers. He knew not only what he was looking for but also where it was — it was in her bedroom.

Kai went to the corner where he thought her bedroom used to be. He looked up and asked, "This is where your bedroom was, right? Was this huge boulder just behind the house, at the corner of your bedroom?"

Leiya affirmed. She pointed to the back wall, showing him where the window was through which she could see the side of the rock, where the bed was, and which side of the bed she got in on.

Kai dropped to his knees in the ash. He started rummaging through the ash and partially burned objects. It wasn't long before he put his hand on it, a flat, wide clay jar. Leiya had kept it under her nightstand. Kai had never seen it before; he'd never been inside Leiya's bedroom. Still, he knew exactly where to look for it.

He pulled it out of the burned debris and walked out of the smoldering remains.

"That's my jewelry jar!"

Kai emptied the contents on the ground.

Leiya gasped for air and fell to her knees next to Kai.

"Oh my!" she exclaimed. "That was my family jewelry!"

Kai picked it up. It was now a warm lump of gold. It was round and roughly flat, about twelve centimeters in diameter and .5 centimeters thick. It wasn't perfectly smooth — the fire had not burned hot or long enough to melt it perfectly. Some fragments were discernible, as were several jewels melted into the gold medallion.

Kai said, "I am so sorry, my love. These must have been important to you."

"This jewelry has been in my family for generations," Leiya whispered. "Look at this," she said as she pointed to one of the jewels. "This was my grandmother's wedding ring."

"And this one," pointing to a chain that hadn't fully melted, "was my great-great-grandmother's. Every mother on my mom's side of the family gave this to their youngest daughter when she became a woman. I was my mother's youngest daughter, so I received it to pass down to my youngest daughter."

Kai said, "This is what we were looking for this morning, isn't it?"

Leiya couldn't speak. She nodded her head yes as tears began pouring down her face.

"I'm so sorry, Leiya," Kai said.

Leiya stuttered in a deep breath. "I am not crying out of sorrow. Not completely anyway. All this loss is sad. But at the same time, I am crying because I feel God's hand on our lives, Kai. I've not lived like this before. It's all so new. And real. What are we experiencing, Kai?"

"God is anointing us for some reason. He must know we need to work for Him and has judged that we will obey Him. That is a lot of responsibility, isn't it?"

She squeezed his hand and repeated a phrase from yesterday, "I believe."

A Burning Question

Hu was already waiting for Maria in the tearoom the following morning.

After Maria sat down, Hu launched into the tea ceremony, as he did yesterday. This time, however, he explained the ceremony's history, showing how many movements were taken from the Catholic celebration of the Eucharist. Christians had developed the tea ceremony to take communion secretly.

Then, Hu began the teaching. "We are on the south scroll, point 1…"

Maria interrupted. "Hu, can I ask you something first?"

"Yes, of course, my daughter."

Maria liked the sound of 'my daughter.' But, she continued with her burning question.

"I need to understand the pendant. I had a dream about it before I knew there was a real one. Then I saw it in real life the next day on Sebastian's neck. I felt connected to this place right away. Then I got freaked out because the dreams continued. Now I'm back, but I feel like there is something in the history here that is mysterious. Who is Leiya? What is the significance of the pendant? Can you tell me what you know?"

Hu looked at her and smiled. He shifted his weight as if to brace his body against the advancement of his family legacy.

"Yes, there is history here. I can fill in a few blanks for you. But allow me to say, you may be disappointed because there is a lot we don't know.

"Let's start with Leiya. She is a woman you would have liked. She was strong, independent, small in stature, huge in heart, beautiful, and discerning when it came to men. She would never marry if she couldn't find a man who would treat her as an equal. This attitude is expected today in the west but was unheard of in seventeenth-century China.

"Leiya fell in love with my ancestor Kai Oda, son of Oda Nobunaga. Kai was everything Leiya wanted in a man. Kai was also a Christian. His brother had developed a unique Asian way to study the Bible called The Tea Room Scrolls, which you are now learning.

"Christianity was not popular in China, and someone who wanted to keep Christianity out of China burned Leiya's house. In the debris, they found a pot of Leiya's gold jewelry that had melted into a medallion. Kai cut it into eight pieces and resolved to teach the Bible throughout Asia. He intended to leave one pendant here, bring one to Japan, and then plant a pendant in six other countries. In each country, the family in which the first tearoom started was supposed to keep the pendant safe, passing it through the generations until, at some point in history, it was supposed to make it back to Japan, where it would be reunited with the others. That was the plan.

Maria asked excitedly, "Can I see the China pendant? I mean, not the replica, but the real thing?"

179

Hu looked pensive. "This is where the story falls apart. We don't know where it is. From what we know, it was carefully preserved in the ground, in or near Leiya's grave, until the early 1800s. At that time, persecutors raided the plantation and killed all three generations who knew the whereabouts of the pendant. The Oda clan in Aomori, Japan, found out, and one of them came in to take over the plantation, but the pendant has never been found. It may be still in the ground, or stolen and sold for its gold value."

"But surely there must be a way to find it? Do we know where the grave site is?"

Maria's curiosity peaked, and she felt compelled to find the pendant. She knew this was a private family matter but couldn't resist pressing the issue.

"Not really. We think we know the general area. And believe me, the location has been searched over and over in the last two hundred years."

"What else do we know?" Maria continued to push like a detective. She felt she had the right; the dreams had invaded her life.

"There are some notes that were preserved. They survived the 1800's massacre. But I am afraid they haven't been helpful. If anything, they have been more perplexing."

"Can I see these notes?"

Hu smiled. "Perhaps. I will pray on that and give God the reigns. He will let me know."

Maria realized she had pushed Hu far enough to make him uncomfortable. "I am sorry, Hu, that I pried into your family matters. And I got us off track. Please continue with your teaching."

"No worries, let's first recap what we talked about yesterday. You are looking for the narrow gate, a spiritual transformation. Remember, Maria, that your greatest pursuits in life will be spiritual. Finding and understanding the golden pendant will be satisfying on one level, but joy is not obtained in physical gold, only in spiritual gold. Turn your thirst to find the narrow gate and then pursue with all your heart the life on the other side of that gate, and you will have found something most people never will: joy that Jesus says is 'life abundant,' joy that the psalmist says is your strength.

"Rise, if you please, and read that little scroll I told you about yesterday. The next scripture we will study is Point One. What does the scroll say?"

Maria stood up and squinted at the tiny scroll within the scroll. "It says, R-O-M 8, colon, 9 dash 17."

"Excellent. Here is a Bible; this is for you to keep. I've already turned to the right place. How about if you read it out loud."

Maria held the Bible, and something changed. She couldn't remember holding a Bible; she had never had a desire. Even as Hu handed it to her, she wasn't sure she wanted to hold one, much less own one.

But now, holding it in her hands, something changed. Her breathing slowed, and her mind settled. She had a peace that she wanted to keep and an assurance she could keep it if she wanted.

Maria sat back on the cushion, put her finger in the Bible to hold her place, and closed it. She touched the cover and ran her hand over it. Her soul connected with it, like sinking into a hot tub.

She pulled her finger out, closed the Bible, and raised it to her chest. She hugged it and started to weep.

Hu watched her reaction and didn't interrupt. He knew what was happening. The Word of God is Jesus. *Physically*, it's a book written by forty men over 1500 years. *Emotionally*, it's a refuge. *Mentally*, it's an intellectual challenge. But **spiritually**, it's Jesus Christ. The proof text is the central verse on the Middle Way Scroll, which Maria had not read nor let Hu read to her. She didn't know this fact, but she didn't need to; she was experiencing the reality firsthand.

Maria looked up at Hu with tears running over her German cheekbones. Looking him in the eyes, she raised the Bible and kissed it. She was trying to tell him something she couldn't understand or put words to, but he already knew.

Hu just smiled. He nodded, "I know, my daughter, I know. And the love story has only begun."

Hu's words struck a cord on the strings of her psyche. She wiped her eyes with a tissue and said, "Hu, teach me this love story. Please. I want to know more. I got a glimpse just now. I want more."

Hu pointed to Maria's Bible. "I'll help you find the place again, and you can read it out loud."

"You, however, are not in the flesh but in the Spirit, if in fact the Spirit of God dwells in you. Anyone who does not have the Spirit of Christ does not belong to him. But if Christ is in you, although the body is dead because of sin, the Spirit is life because of righteousness. If the Spirit of him who raised

Jesus from the dead dwells in you, he who raised Christ Jesus from the dead will also give life to your mortal bodies through the Spirit who dwells in you."

"So then, brothers, we are debtors, not to the flesh, to live according to the flesh. For if you live according to the flesh you will die, but if by the Spirit you put to death the deeds of the body, you will live. For all who are led by the Spirit of God are sons of God. For you did not receive the spirit of slavery to fall back into fear, but you have received the Spirit of adoption as sons, by whom we cry, 'Abba! Father!' The Spirit himself bears witness with our spirit that we are children of God, and if children, then heirs—heirs of God and fellow heirs with Christ, provided we suffer with him in order that we may also be glorified with him."

Hu said, "Humans are uniquely positioned within the animal kingdom. We have conscious choice. As discussed yesterday, one of the choices we have is which gate to go through. Today, we see that this choice determines whether the Spirit of God lives in us. This scripture describes our selection as living in the flesh or God's Spirit. Living in the flesh is a euphemism for living to please ourselves. Living in the Spirit is living to please the Spirit of God.

"Some people think Christians are told to follow a list of rules. But Jesus doesn't say that. We are given a choice. And along with the choice, He gives us sufficient advice regarding His suggested path. Selfish living feels good for a season, but it leads to "slavery," according to this scripture. Living in the Spirit, alternatively, leads to life. It's a joy that you will know. In fact, you just got a dose of that joy. God's grace came over you, and you experienced what it feels like to be in his stream of love. It can take a little while for a Christian to practice living in that joy because God leaves it to us to pursue. But when He sees we are serious about seeking His joy, ways, and will, He draws closer to us and fills us with His joy."

Hu continued to teach Maria about this scripture. Eventually, he asked her a question.

He pointed to the words, *received the Spirit of adoption*, and asked, "Would you like to receive the Spirit of adoption?"

Maria sat still. Her immediate thought was affirmative. She had just experienced the most exquisite love, and she wanted more. But it sounded strange, almost spooky, to receive a spirit of adoption.

She sat still for a moment, weighing things in her mind. She was tired of feeling like a scared little girl. She had come to China knowing something had to be missing from her life. Years of empty, unfulfilled, partly cloudy skies had built up frustration. Her whole being cried out, "YES, I WANT *THE* MORE!!"

Yet every time she came close, she got scared and retreated.

Furthermore, she reasoned, this was not spooky or a cult. These were Jesus' words, not Hu's or his ancestors or somebody on a street corner.

She liked that she was *not* being told she "had to, or else..." She was free to walk away, as she did before. She intuitively knew this was right, warm, loving, kind, and a free choice.

Moreover, asking to be adopted by the God who created her made sense. She had never felt entirely alone; she wasn't homeless like the people living on the streets of Frankfurt. But, she had always said that if she were really in trouble, she would cry out to the God with the most power; she was going straight to the top.

Hu knew she was processing everything and sensed some reticence, so he finally said, "Maria, Jesus will not force himself upon you. He didn't do that during His earthly ministry, and He isn't doing that with you now. God loves you so much, Maria, that He gives you the free will to decide whether you want to be a part of His people, an adopted daughter. Do you think you want this now or would you feel more comfortable…"

"Yes," Maria interrupted. "More than anything. I want to grow as close to Jesus as I can."

"Then you'll need to pray for yourself."

Hu saw bewilderment in Maria's face and continued, "There is no magic prayer, only that you have to ask God yourself. He answers the prayers of His sincere followers. I can help you this time. But you will need to keep praying something similar, frequently asking for Him to change you into the daughter He wants you to be.

"Close your eyes and repeat after me. Heavenly Father, as the God who created me and the universe, I ask you to adopt me as your daughter. Have mercy on me. I have lived my life ignoring you, being my own god and master. I have strayed from what you have wanted for me out of ignorance. I have now changed my mind. And I am asking you to change my ways to the ways of Christ. I don't want to live by the flesh, as this scripture says; I want to live by the Spirit. I receive the Spirit of adoption, the Spirit of Christ, to help me live as you will, not by my will. I want to spend every day growing as close as possible to You. I surrender everything I am to you, God. As your daughter, having received the Spirit of adoption, I am giving you complete control. I receive and ask that you change me, transform me into the daughter you designed me to be. Amen."

Maria opened her eyes with a smile and a tear rolling down her cheek. Hu opened his arms, and Maria melted into him. She felt good,

185

right, relieved, and comforted. She knew she had just decided to change the course of her life.

Later, when Maria was in the car with Martin, she told him that she prayed to receive the Spirit of Christ and asked God to adopt her as a daughter.

Martin was excited for her.

They spent hours talking that day as they ran errands. Martin talked about Jesus like a best friend. He prayed for people as they passed them on the street. He helped people in the stores. He spoke kindly to every clerk. He lived his faith openly, causing Maria to wince the first time he said to a clerk he didn't know, "Thank you. Praise Jesus!" In a town of few Christians, it seemed like he was out of place. And yet, everyone seemed to like him. Nobody reacted negatively; to the contrary, he seemed to brighten their day. Martin's faith was his life. He was drawn to God, and people were drawn to him. Maria had to admit that she found it attractive.

Eventually, later in the afternoon, Maria and Martin found themselves parked at the port and walking barefoot along the beach. Martin asked a question.

"What do you want to do with the rest of your life?" he asked.

Maria turned her head and stared off across the sea. "I don't know," she responded. "So much has changed in just three days at the campground. I'm now open to so much I have never thought about before. I can tell you one thing; I want to find that missing pendant. I talked to your dad about it today. It's hard to get my mind off it."

Maria turned her head and looked back towards Martin. "How about you? What do you want?" she asked.

"I want to spend the rest of my life introducing others to Jesus," he said excitedly. "You know that feeling you described while praying with my dad this morning? I want to spend forever leading others to that same experience, something they will remember for the rest of their lives."

Maria laughed and hit him on the shoulder playfully. "I just said I wanted to solve a mystery about a missing piece of jewelry, and you gave a much more lofty and worthy answer. Martin, *how* do I find the same excitement you have for God?"

"Maybe they are related, I don't know. But the answer is to spend as much time as you can in your Bible," Martin told her.

"The Bible," he continued, as he picked up a rock and skipped it across the bay water, "says that faith comes by hearing and hearing by the word of Christ. That is how you build intimacy with Jesus; it's one of the top five teachings of Jesus."

"I'll remember that," Maria replied.

It was quiet for about 50 yards on the beach before Maria broke the silence.

"Speaking of intimacy," she said, "do you have a girlfriend, or are you seeing someone?"

"I haven't been on a date in over a year," he answered. "I guess I don't get away from the plantation enough."

"Why is that?" Maria questioned.

"I've always believed that the plantation would play a significant role with the woman I marry. It's something that has repeated itself throughout my family's history. My dad worked at the campground when my mom came on a camping trip. It's how they met. Back to when the scrolls and the tea house first became a part of the plantation, relationships that begin at the plantation lead to marriages that last a lifetime."

"We met at the plantation," Maria joked.

Martin laughed. "But what about you? Do you have anyone special in your life?"

"Nope," Maria assured him. "Just you and your dad, and I'm pretty sure he's taken."

The two laughed aloud as they continued down the beach heading back towards Martin's truck. Martin slowly started moving in closer to Maria as they walked. Their hands touched, and he reached for hers. He looked at her as they continued walking, ensuring the hand holding was okay. She drew closer to him, touching shoulder to shoulder, and leaning her head into him.

The Great Unifier, In Japan Again

Within a few months, Kai and Leiya were married, their new home was finished a short walk from the tea house, and the plantation was hitting the year's busy season. Not only had several new workers moved onto the plantation, but more and more were surrendering their lives to Jesus and learning the Bible through the Tea Room Scrolls.

There was no more trouble from Yìchén and his men. Kai and Leiya had even regularly started making trips to Ningde without fear of who might recognize them. The plantation was no longer only known as somewhere a person could go for work or a new start in life. People from the village heard about the tea house and went to the plantation simply to learn from the scrolls.

One afternoon, Kai and Leiya were finishing an afternoon walk when one of the workers came yelling for Leiya.

Kai's heart sunk in his chest. He was instantly reminded of the evening Hàoyǔ was screaming for them because the house had been set on fire. Kai braced himself for trouble as the worker yelling for them came into view.

"Leiya," the young man excitedly exclaimed. "Come quick. We've been looking for you."

"What is it?" Laiya answered.

189

"It's your sister," the worker informed her. "Ju is here and is waiting to see you."

Leiya turned and looked at Kai as excitement began to take over. She hadn't seen her older sister in over five years.

The resemblance between Leiya and her older sister Ju was obvious. Same cheekbones, braided hair, quick to smile, and high intelligence. Growing up, the two girls had been close. They shared the same need for independence—they wanted to learn everything for themselves, experience everything on their own and accomplish everything by themselves.

They were both driven to achieve. Kai had seen Leiya's drive in how she ran a successful plantation. And now he could see it in Ju's pursuits as well. Ju might have taken over the plantation if she hadn't fallen in love with a different business, the import/export business. Kai was delighted to share stories with Ju about some of the same people they knew in the ports around Asia. Ju had traveled the world and managed to make a lot of money doing so.

"I've been in Borneo for five years. I went there because I thought I had fallen in love, but it didn't work out. I'm getting older and considering coming home to my roots. I know this may be taking you by surprise, but Leiya, I was thinking of returning to the plantation. You would still run the plantation, Leiya. This is yours. But maybe I could help? Maybe I could open up some new markets for you?"

Ju had never been married. As an attractive and intelligent woman who always managed to find a way of her own, she had the same opinion about marriage as Leiya. She wanted a man who would love her as an equal. She was content to live without a man, if she couldn't find what she believed was right.

"How have things been on the financial end of the plantation?" Ju asked her younger sister once they were sitting at the fire.

"We make things work," Leiya answered. "Yes, money is important to meet the needs of caring for the plantation. Still, for the last several years, my focus has been on using the plantation to create a new life for the workers. Many people here would be lost with nowhere else to go without the plantation providing for them."

Leiya paused to take a sip of tea.

"As long as we can provide a comfortable place for the workers to be, the plantation has been considered successful," Leiya continued.

"I get it," Ju interrupted. "You have grown up exactly like mom. The well-being of others will always come before your gain. Still, what if you could make more profit, expand the plantation, and help even more people? Would you want to do that?"

Ju went silent, looking at Kai and Leiya as they pondered what they heard.

"What exactly do you have in mind?" Leiya asked.

"You know the alpine plants we have? What if we marketed them as a specialty tea?"

Ju leaned forward, placing her elbows on her knees. "You know the flavor is uniquely divine, but we've never marketed it with a specialty image. We've concentrated on the seasoned by fire tea. But those alpine plants produce a delicious cup of tea that cannot be found anywhere in the markets. I know I could sell it, Leiya, even if we charged five times the price."

"I have been looking for a way to give Hàoyǔ more responsibility," Leiya said as she turned her head towards Kai. "He has learned the entire operation already. Maybe he could be in charge of this initiative and work directly with Ju."

It didn't take long for Ju and Hàoyǔ to expand demand and profits. With the increased profits, they purchased adjacent land and developed the plantation.

The plantation was bringing in more money than it had in years. The number of workers spending time at the tea house and learning the scrolls was continually growing.

Kai and Leiya grew as a couple, a man and woman of God, and then as parents. Genghis had Leiya's light eyebrows, the dimples in her cheeks, and the longer chin Kai had from his mother's side of the family. Life was full and wonderful.

But Kai knew the winds of change were blowing. This sweet and contented life was not what God portrayed in Leiya's dream. Nobumasa had also told him, long before he came to China, that he believed God had anointed him uniquely. Nobumasa had said, "Not everyone is asked to make an equal sacrifice; yours could be more than most, my brother."

"Close your eyes for a few minutes while I share something with you," Kai told her.

"It was during your second or third month of pregnancy God started to do some tugging on my heart. He reminded me of the mission He has for our family, sharing the Gospel and the Tea Room Scrolls; it extends much further than the boundaries of the plantation."

Kai then placed eight pendants in Leiya's hands; each had a hole fashioned in the top to accommodate a chain to make it a necklace.

Leiya opened her eyes. "They're so beautiful, Kai. How did you get these?"

Before he could respond, Leiya said, "Oh wait! This is my jewelry, right?"

"Yes, I made them. Each was cut from the disk of melted jewelry we found after the house burned. Like the tea that has financially blessed our plantation, these pendants have been seasoned by fire."

"There are eight pendants, each representing a place our family is to share the Gospel message. One will stay here in China, one will go to Japan to be at the Onsen, and the other six will be spread to where God will lead me.

"Eventually, probably long after I die, all eight of these pendants will be rejoined in Japan, where all of this started, where my father's legacy remains, and where God gave my brother a uniquely Asian way to study the Bible.

"My father, Oda Nobunaga, is known as the greatest samurai who ever lived because he unified Japan like no other leader in Japan's history. This was good. Yet, God has an even greater legacy attached to the Oda name. Our family's mission is to unify Japan again, this time under Christ."

Leiya inspected several of the pieces. "Oh, I see! You cut them imperfectly, so they go back together in only one way."

Kai nodded as Leiya put all eight pieces next to each other in the correct order, so they formed a disk again.

"Is this to signify unification?"

"Yes, it is Leiya. I believe God wants Jesus to come back to Japan. We kicked Him out and murdered the Christians, not unlike Jesus' parable of the tenants. But God is sure to forgive and does not hold us responsible for the actions of our fathers. He dearly loves the people of Japan."

"One day, in His timing, the people of Japan will find their way back to their Creator. I pray it is sooner rather than later, but His will be done on earth as it is in heaven. He doesn't give us any more information than we need. And right now, He's told me to preach the gospel in six other Asian countries. And I've said, "Yes, Lord, send me.""

It's Here Somewhere

The following week flew by. Mornings were spent with Hu in the tea house, learning the south scroll. In the afternoons and evenings Maria hung out with Martin. As much as she learned from Hu about Jesus and the Bible, Maria also learned from Martin.

"What happens now?" Maria asked Hu. They had worked through the south scroll and finished the final point the morning before. Maria had woken up that morning and headed to the tea house like she'd done every day since being at the plantation. It had become routine over the past weeks. Maria was already waking up several minutes before her alarm clock would ring in the mornings.

"What do you want to happen now?" Hu asked her.

Maria sat on a stump next to Hu at the fire ring outside the tea house. Every morning, the two spent time around a small fire before heading into the tea house.

"I haven't wanted to intrude on the ancient notes you have on the pendant. I asked about it a while ago, and you said, 'Maybe.' I am sorry to bring it up again. But to give you an honest answer to your question, what I would like to do next is investigate the missing pendant. Would I be out of line to ask again?"

"I've been praying about that, asking God for His wisdom. I don't feel like I have confirmation yet. But I trust God has an answer for me."

"Well, in the meantime, I don't want this to be over," Maria said.

Hu's big smile started to grow across his face. "Have you asked God if He has a specific reason for you returning to Frankfurt as a believer?"

"No, I haven't," Maria confessed. "I haven't thought about what it would be like as a believer anywhere. I guess I wasn't thinking about being anywhere but here."

Hu said, "Let's both pray and ask God for His guidance on the next step. The Bible says that if we seek wisdom, we should ask, and He will grant it. So let's spend a couple of days praying about this."

Maria leaned her head to the side and looked at Hu. "I like that idea," she said with a smile.

That night, Maria changed into pajamas and laid down in bed for the night. She prayed, asking God to reveal her next steps. It didn't take long for her to fall asleep.

Maria watched as Hu bent over, searching through the grass along a tree line. "Are you sure I can't help?" she asked him.

"No, that's alright," he replied. "You don't know what I'm looking for. But, I promise you," Hu continued, "this will change the rest of your life. When we find this, nothing is ever going to be the same. This is part of your purpose in life, Maria."

As more and more time went by, Maria started becoming impatient. It seemed like Hu had been searching on the ground for hours.

Maria took a couple of steps backward and then looked at the sky. Her focus had been on Hu watching him search the ground. It wasn't until she looked up that Maria realized where they were. They were searching at the campsite where she and Sebastian had stayed her first night at the campground. Hu was close to where Maria had pitched her tent.

"This was the original location of the tea house," Hu explained. "As the campground grew over the years, the tea room was moved to where it sits now. Here is where Kai originally started teaching the Tea Room Scrolls at the plantation. My father was the first in our family to make this area available to campers."

"Remind me who Kai is?" Maria asked.

"He is my ancestor. Kai was the first of our family to move here from Japan. He was introduced to Jesus by his brother. He had the purpose of spreading the Gospel and teaching the scrolls throughout Asia."

"It's here somewhere," Hu exclaimed. "But now, you have to find it. Your destiny and place in my family can't be carried out until you do. Finding this will show me that you and Martin must make your way to Japan!"

"Why would the two of us leave for Japan?" Maria wanted to know.

"To reunite this pendant with the others," he answered. "You finding this will confirm what the Holy Spirit has told me about you."

Maria sat straight up in her bed. She wiped her eyes as if trying to clear a haze. Maria quickly climbed out of bed and kneeled on the floor, bowing her head in prayer.

"Heavenly Father, clear my mind and help me recall what I just dreamed. If you have a plan and purpose for me here at the plantation, show me in a way that will erase all doubt and uncertainty. I'm willing to follow wherever it is you want to guide me. I just have to know that you are the one guiding the way. Amen."

Maria finished with the journaling and then grabbed her phone. It was just after 1:00 a.m. She didn't want to risk waking Hu, but he had instructed her to inform him immediately if the dreams returned. So she opened the text thread and sent Hu a message.

"I had another dream," was all it said.

As soon as Maria placed the phone on the table, it started vibrating.

"I had one also," Hu replied. "Is it ok if I come to talk to you?"

"I'd like that," she replied.

He knocked on the cabin door less than 10 minutes later.

"Let's sit on the porch and talk for a few minutes," Hu suggested. The two sat down next to each other on the steps leading up to the porch.

"Why don't you tell me about your dream first, and then I'll tell you about mine," he said.

Maria went over the details of her dream. Maria described where the two of them were in the dream and the proximity to her tent. She then told Hu what he had said to her in the dream. The details about Kai were important. She thought Hu's comment about Maria's destiny and place in the family was equally significant.

Hu listened to everything Maria had to say without interrupting.

He turned his head and looked off into the dark of the night once he was confident Maria had finished.

"I've had occasional dreams like that for the last thirty years," Hu admitted.

"It had been a long time, though. Until the night after you and I first met. That night, not only did I have a dream about the pendant, but I had a dream about you," he continued.

"What was it about?" Maria questioned.

"Our family had always believed one of the original pendants stayed here at the plantation before Kai left for Japan. He brought the Japan pendant directly to Oda Onsen. And the other six were brought to other countries where Kai taught the Bible using the Tea Room Scrolls. Eventually, each of the eight pendants was to find their way back to Japan at the right time.

"I dreamed that you had found the missing pendant. And after finding the pendant, you and Martin made plans to take it to the land of my ancestors in Japan."

Hu smiled. "I brought you a copy of our family notes regarding the pendant. This copy is yours. I was waiting for confirmation from God. God gave me the assurance that I should share them with you."

God's Grace

Do you hear that?" Kai asked one day as he and Leiya were approaching the edge of the woods finishing their walk.

Leiya stopped walking and focused on the noise of their surroundings. "Hear what?" she asked. "It sounds quiet to me."

"Exactly," Kai told her. "Almost too quiet. We should be able to hear the business of the plantation."

The three hurried out of the woods towards their house with Genghis asleep in the pack on Kai's back. No sound of workers talking and communicating amongst themselves. The closer Kai and Leiya got to their home, the more deserted it looked.

Leiya took Genghis into the house to put him in his bed, while Kai went to the distribution building, looking for an explanation. No workers were finishing the day's responsibilities.

"Hàoyǔ," Kai yelled as loud as he could, hoping his friend could hear and explain what was happening. After a few minutes walking around the plantation and not seeing anyone, Kai ran towards the house. Something was wrong. Not a single person responded to his yells for Hàoyǔ or made themselves available to Kai.

Kai walked through the front door and was overcome with fear and disbelief. There stood Leiya, Ju, and Hàoyǔ, surrounded by Yìchén and ten of his men. In Yìchén's arms was his son, Genghis.

"If you're any kind of a man, you will let them all go and take me," Kai said.

Yìchén tilted his head back, crying out in laughter.

"Any kind of a man?" Yìchén asked. "I'm the kind of man standing here with complete control of your wife, son, and closest friends."

Yìchén took a few steps towards Kai, pointing at him with one hand while holding Genghis in the other. "If you were any kind of a man, you would have never put them in this position."

Suddenly, Hàoyǔ bolted towards Yìchén. Two of the other men quickly grabbed him before he could do anything. It was a fool's errand; they were far outnumbered. Yìchén had the upper hand.

The noise and commotion startled Genghis. He started crying loudly. Leiya instinctively went to get to her son, but another of Yìchén's men stepped in the way, forcibly knocking Leiya to the ground.

Kai stood motionless, watching the scene. Kai knew he needed to wait. He prayed and asked God to bring in the workers from the field. They needed to even the playing field.

"That's enough," Kai exclaimed. "Let them go. I'm the one you want. Get your men together, and I'll leave with you. You win. I'll go wherever you want. Just leave them alone."

"You are partially correct," Yìchén replied. "Yes, because of how you disrespected me in my own home, I want to inflict great pain on you.

But, more than that, because of what you believe in, I want everyone you may have influenced with your Christianity nonsense to see where your faith will lead them."

Yìchén turned around, looking at the men he had with him in the room. "He's right," Yìchén exclaimed. "That's enough, at least inside of the house anyway. Let's join everyone else and make sure they watch how great Kai's God is."

Yìchén and his men led the way outside and towards the housing buildings on the plantation. Yìchén called out loud for another man who wasn't in the group when they were close enough to the facilities for him to hear.

"Bring all of them," Yìchén ordered. "If anyone resists or tries to get away, have your men kill them on the spot. Let them know that all we want is for them to watch. Then, they will be free to leave when we're finished."

It was finally clear why Kai could not find any of the workers. Yìchén had brought a small army with him, and they held the plantation workers in one of the outbuildings. One had already been killed, setting an example of what would happen if anyone tried to resist or flee.

All the workers were gathered in a large group in the open.

Kai was put on his knees, facing the group of workers with everyone's attention. Still holding Genghis in his arms, Yìchén approached Kai from his side. Yìchén kicked him as hard as he could in the chest, knocking Kai backward onto the ground.

Yìchén said, loud enough for everyone in the group to hear him, "I'm fully aware that not all of you know what has been taught on this plantation about the Christian faith. Since I have no way of knowing which of you believes in Jesus, I want to make sure everyone sees the consequences of getting led astray by a foreign religion."

"This man has tried to convince many of you that if you believe in Jesus Christ, you will have everlasting life. I will show you just how long that life will last."

Yìchén took several running steps and kicked Kai in the ribs with all his force. Kai shrieked in pain, pulling his knees as close to his chin as he could. Then Yìchén kicked him in the face, holding the crying baby the whole time.

"Get up on your knees and look," Yìchén screamed at Kai. "You are the one with the most to learn. You are the one who is going to watch."

"Bring me his wife," Yìchén demanded.

One of his men brought Leiya and stood beside Kai. Yìchén handed the baby to the man and took hold of Leiya's hair, yanking her around to face the crowd.

"It is said that you can cut a person a thousand times before they bleed out and die," Yìchén said, loud enough for everyone to hear while keeping his eyes fixed on Kai. "I don't think she'll last that long."

He pulled a knife with a six-inch blade from a sheath.

"Not only are you going to watch," Yìchén said while pointing the knife at Kai, "you are going to count out loud so we don't lose track of the count. If you don't count, your son will get the cuts until you remember what number we are on. I want you to see firsthand just

203

how everlasting a Christian life is. But it gets better. You are going to count from the cross."

Kai looked over to see two of Yìchén's men bringing a cross toward them. Yìchén had his men tie Kai to the cross. They had already dug a hole, and Kai was soon hoisted up to be crucified.

Kai thought about his brother, Nobumasa, who had narrowly escaped crucifixion. He thought about Jesus on the cross, and realized that the sinners were beneath him from this vantage point. He saw them as God sees them. Lost, angry, and at war with Him. He thought about all the conversations he wanted to have with them, to help them find peace with their Creator. He silently prayed for each of them as the strength drained from his arms.

The men tied Leiya down to a table in front of the cross. Kai and Leiya could see each other. Kai expressed his undying love for her.

She said, "I love you, Kai. I still believe you have work to do. But, not our will, only His. I will see you soon. I am going to be with my Savior now."

She closed her eyes and started to pray.

From the first cut, Leiya never whimpered or cried. She knew the Kingdom of God had descended on her, just as Jesus promised in the beatitudes. She was a living witness to Matthew 5:10 — "Blessed are those who are persecuted because of righteousness, for theirs is the kingdom of heaven." Leiya was indeed being blessed; a peaceful smile never left her face, reminding Kai of Steven's stoning recounted in the Bible.

Kai was forced to keep the count, desperately fighting off unconsciousness. He knew the evil in Yìchén would turn against his son if he didn't keep the count. All Kai had left to protect was Genghis; he and Leiya were both hopelessly slipping towards death.

Leiya continued to pray, out loud. She prayed forgiveness over the persecutors. She prayed for Genghis and Kai. She prayed for every worker who was witnessing the evil.

The more she prayed, the angrier and more violent Yìchén reacted. It didn't take long for her spirit to pass into Jesus' arms.

Leiya's passing made it easier for Kai to relax into unconsciousness. Kai's body intermittently fell limp, then stuttered awake to take breath into his suffocating lungs.

While they waited for Kai die, Yìchén's men burned every building on the plantation. Every worker's clothes and possessions were thoroughly incinerated. Yìchén made sure there was no reason for anyone to want to return. Moreover, he didn't want a trace to be left of the Christian faith taught at the plantation.

After it was obvious Kai had deceased, the workers were told to leave the plantation as quickly as possible if they didn't want to experience the same fate as Kai and his wife.

When freed, they took off running as fast as possible. A few headed for the woods but most ran for the gate. They ran toward the setting sun as if to keep it from leaving them. Wiggly long shadows trailed behind, reminding them that their minds would never forget this shade of evil.

Hàoyǔ went to the woods and didn't slow down until he was at the tea house. Because Yìchén's men didn't realize how far into the woods the property extended, the tea house was the only building that hadn't been set on fire.

It was soon quiet, eerily so. Though evil had already come, darkness descended.

Walking out of the woods, Hàoyǔ saw a scene that would haunt him for years to come.

A full moon lighted the plantation just above the horizon. Multiple wisps of smoke were pluming up through the sky as if they were compelled to find God because the earth was such a vile place.

Still on the cross, Kai was silhouetted, perfectly centered against the round, pale orange moon. Below Kai, Leiya's lifeless body laid flat, arms splayed out over the sides of the table to which she was still strapped.

Hàoyǔ remembered talking with Kai about the Valley of Hinnom, a place where the Jews burned garbage in endless fires, a veritable hell on earth.

He shivered.

It took superhuman strength for Hàoyǔ to get the cross out of the hole. Once on the ground, Hàoyǔ untied Kai's hands and feet from the wooden cross.

Hàoyǔ kneeled on the ground and laid his hands on Kai's chest. Then, with tears, he quietly cried, "Why, God?"

Hàoyǔ thought he felt a slight movement in Kai's chest. He turned him onto his side and got a muffled cough. Then a fresh stream of blood trickled out of Kai's mouth.

"Kai," Hàoyǔ anxiously said. "Can you hear me, Kai?"

Hàoyǔ leaned down to Kai's ear and whispered loud enough for his friend to hear, "I'm right here. I've got you."

Hàoyǔ continued to encourage his friend back to life, "Just breathe, Kai. Everyone is gone. Cough and breathe as loud as you need to."

"Leiya?" Kai whispered.

I Will Replay That In My Mind Forever

That night, and for the next several days, Maria devoured the ancient notes. They were clear in some places and cryptic in others. For example, Hàoyǔ had detailed notes on the attack in 1627 that killed Leiya, and Kai nearly.

But the description of the location of Leiya's grave and the pendant was not as clear. The only notes on the grave were given in a diagram meant to help locate the unmarked grave. The drawing was a simple triangle with distances. The third point of the triangle was marked "Grave." The other two points were unmarked.

Without knowing the other two points, finding the grave was hopeless.

Maria surmised that the other two points must have been significant and evident to those in the past.

Hu was able to share some additional information. One theory was that one of the markers was the site of Kai's crucifixion. And that site was marked by a stone cross in the ground.

Maria, Martin, and Hu found the stone cross in the ground. It was a crude cross made of three stones. Two stones made a "T" and a smaller third stone, placed on the top, completed the cross.

It was a start. Maria slept soundly that night, knowing they had one point of three.

The next day, Martin asked Maria to take a walk with him. "I want to show you my favorite place on the plantation."

They talked and walked up to the highest point of the plantation. When they reached the top, Maria was surprised tea plants could grow in those conditions.

Maria shivered and said, "Now I know why you told me to bring an extra shirt."

Martin said, "Yes, isn't it amazing up here? It is a different growing zone. The weather is much cooler here, nearly every day. This is where Leiya pulled tea plants to send to Japan. Nobumasa needed the cultivar that could grow in these alpine conditions. These plants are different and produce a unique flavor, reminiscent of a Darjeeling but a little fruitier. And unlike Darjeeling, this tea can be steeped longer without getting bitter."

"I don't think I've had any of this tea, Martin; I always had the smoky tea. Remind me when we get down; I want to try it."

Martin said, "I will. I believe we have a little private stash at home. Lately, we have smoked this cultivar for several years because demand is so high for the Seasoned by Fire tea. It's a shame because when this tea is air dried, it is a sparkling gem among Chinese teas."

The top of the plantation was open to the north, and a breeze was blowing in from this direction, bringing with it wisps of wet, drizzly clouds. The clouds rolled up the mountain's north side and hit the southern air currents rising from the valley. At the intersection, the clouds dissipated. Cloudy on one side, sunny on the other. It was a special place, mystical even.

They walked the cloudy ridge along a tea picking trail until the view opened to the campsite and plantation buildings below.

"Oh, this is spectacular, Martin!" In her delight, she reached back for his hand and drew him into her.

Martin snuggled into Maria and hugged her from behind. He lowered his voice, speaking softly into her ear. "I know. Isn't this a magnificent place?"

"It's so beautiful here. You waited a long time for me to see this."

Martin's arms were wrapped around Maria, and her arms were over his, holding him to her. She squeezed tighter to assure him he was doing the right thing by getting this close to her.

"I waited for a reason. I wanted to ensure that we were in my favorite place on earth the first time I kissed you."

Maria released her arms and turned to face him. She looked up into his eyes. She felt right. Here, on a mountain in China, her life was changing rapidly. And she wanted all these changes. She had come to China looking for passion, something that took her breath away, to dislodge the stale air stuck in her lungs for twenty-one years. She'd found Jesus, and now Martin.

"Are you asking permission to kiss me?" She reached up and ran her fingers through his jet-black hair. At the back of his head, she caressed and gently nudged him closer till his lips were just an inch apart from hers.

He spoke to her, up closer than she had let anyone. Previously, she would have found it too close, too invasive. But now, her passion was boiling inside, wondering when he would close the gap.

"Yes, I am asking permission to kiss you, Maria. I want to kiss you on this mountain where the sun meets the clouds. Where two ecosystems meet, mix, and bear fruit of a special kind. May I kiss you, my sweetness?"

Maria couldn't hold back any longer. She closed the gap, kissing him with years of love held behind a dam. It was time for the love to flow freely, down the mountain, into Martin's valley.

Martin responded, and they kissed passionately. The land seemed to rise from the valley to tell him it was time. The Holy Spirit was speaking directly to Martin, almost like a voice rising from the valley. She is the one, the Holy Spirit said. You persevered for the right one. You found her. You waited the right time to receive confirmation, and now you've kissed her. She is yours. You are hers.

But, all things in due time, the Holy Spirit seemed to add. The Oda Valley follows God's wisdom. There is a commitment order. There is a right way to proceed to make it truly last. Follow my wisdom, written across the ages, from the prophets to those who have ears to hear. Stay true to the path of wisdom, my son.

They stopped, and Maria gently turned to the vista, still snuggled into his arms.

Maria spoke softly, "Martin, I think I am falling for you. In fact, I know I am. But I need to take everything slowly. Are you okay with that?"

She didn't wait for him to respond. She spun around and quickly kissed his lips before he could say anything.

She looked at him after the kiss and said, "I'm not telling you we've already gone too fast. I will replay that first kiss in my mind forever. I just need..."

"I know," Martin interrupted. "Me too. Your pace is perfect for me. It's God's pace. We need to stay in step with Him. We'll know when to go further. And ultimately, I need to stay within God's wise counsel. I have been saving my...uh...for marriage."

She was delighted. She turned back to the view. "Me too. I wasn't following God's counsel, though. I didn't know Him. I just knew I didn't want it until it was right. Men have ridiculed me, which only proved my position. Even my girlfriends didn't understand. But I have always felt that my intimacy *is mine*; I should choose wisely because the heart and intimacy go together. Giving one without the other seems disjointed. In my imagination, I saw myself regretting a decision to give my heart and intimacy to someone who *only* wanted to give me intimacy in return—a recipe for heart sickness. I believe it leads to a society of women and men who undervalue their hearts. If we undervalue our intimacy, we will undervalue our hearts. They are inextricably tied together, so if we undervalue one, we will undervalue the other. This is a tragedy on a personal level, but look what it did to Greece, Rome, and many other cultures. Crash and burn, eventually."

Martin smiled. "Wow, that was fantastic. Truly. Bravo! I said, 'Follow God.' But you just gave a short diatribe that sums up, in secular terms, the folly of modern society."

She turned back around and kissed him again. "I believe. I believe you that God knows what is best. Let's live our lives now to the fullest. I am happiest with you. I love being around you. I love sharing my thoughts and knowing I am safe. Truly, I love myself best with you. I know God will carry us forward in His timing, His will, and His ways. And to quote my man, "Praise Jesus!"

He laughed.

There was a bench nearby, and they sat together.

Maria pointed down into the valley. "Hey, you can see our flag on the crucifixion site. The grave site must be that way, right?"

"Yes," Martin agreed, following her hand to the right.

"But," Martin pointed his arm back to the left, "the problem is we don't know if the second point is above the cross or below the cross."

"You are right. I guess I intuitively felt it was above. But," Maria hesitated, "I thought your dad said that the grave site was believed to be over there in those trees and hills to the right. That's over at the very edge of the valley, in the campground."

"Yes, that's correct. There is one campsite that is just above the valley on a little knoll—I think that is the site you stayed at when you first came here. It's on that knoll that her grave was thought to be. Measurements we have used in the past led us there. And, we know her grave site is above the valley because of some notes left by Hàoyǔ; he references a conversation with Kai on a visit back to the plantation, in which he says they were at the grave site "overlooking the plantation." But the site has been searched carefully over the centuries—nothing has been found."

Maria's mathematical mind was humming. "Okay, then the point of the triangle at the cross must be the lower point of the triangle.

Otherwise, if we extended the triangle with the cross at the top point, the grave site would be way down there, in the flats. Right?"

"I think you are right, Maria. Okay, let's assume the cross is the lower point of the triangle; it looks like the upper side would be over near those boulders?"

"You could be right." Maria twisted around on the bench and popped to her feet. "Come. Let's go measure it!"

When they returned to the valley, Martin found a 25-meter tape measure. They carefully measured the distance from the cross's center to the boulder's highest point. 91.8 meters.

They brought out the family notes, and the length was recorded as .158 li. Li is a measurement of distance, sometimes known as the Chinese Mile.

Hu joined them at about this time and noted that an expert was hired many years ago. He assured them that while the li changed in length over the dynasties and was remarkably fluid during the Ming dynasty, this region was remote and slow to change. It never changed the length of li from the previous dynasty (Northern Song) to the subsequent dynasty (Qing). Therefore, all through the Ming dynasty, which was the dynasty in 1627-29, the li was the same measurement.

"But," Hu added, "unfortunately, we've never been able to make sense of the distances. The top of the triangle seems to go from the cross to the top of the biggest boulder. But, unfortunately, it doesn't work."

Maria quickly calculated it and agreed. It didn't work. The map said .158 li, but they came up with .203 li. It was off significantly.

Maria was disappointed.

Hu could see her deflated look. "Don't be too disappointed! Our family has been trying to figure this out for two centuries. But, we are taking a fresh look now."

He pointed back out toward the flag at the cross. "When you look, shortening this distance by 25% leaves us in an area that makes no sense. Even still, we've tried looking for other markers at that distance, in both directions, but with no luck. This boulder and the cross are natural and obvious markers, but one of them has to be wrong."

Maria slept well that night, until 2 am, when she woke from a dream. In her dream, she was riding on a playground merry-go-round in Germany. She was getting sick from going around repeatedly. The older kids wouldn't let her off, though, so she sat in the middle, with no way off. Finally, a parent told the other kids to stop and let her off.

She got off, dizzy, hardly able to stand. The parent, who now looked like a Chinese man, told her in Mandarin, "You need to remember that circles are *measured* by 360 degrees. *Measured.*" He emphasized the word measured twice.

When she woke up, she imagined the bed was going round and round. Her heart started to pick up. She touched her foot to the ground to clear the dream from her mind. Convinced she was grounded, with no spinning, she got out of bed.

She saw the notes on the table. They were drawing her in like a bug to a light. But in the fog of a 2 am mind, she felt that if she went to them, she would feel the disappointment a bug feels — that the light wasn't as interesting as she hoped.

215

When she couldn't sleep at her parent's house, she would sit at the puzzle table. Her mom always had a jigsaw puzzle going. Maria would do the puzzle for a couple of hours until she felt tired again.

She sat down at the table with the Oda Plantation notes. There was nothing else to do; this was her jigsaw puzzle tonight.

She started reading from the beginning again.

Hàoyǔ had written detailed notes about the first time he met Kai in Shanghai, their dangerous journey, rescues, and painful recoveries. He described Leiya, her family, and the admirable purpose of the plantation. He described the tea process and the plantation dimensions, complete with a diagram with distances outlining the entire plantation and building dimensions. From there, he told the love story between Kai and Leiya, the trip to Japan, the return to Ningde, the altercation with Yìchén, and the first attack on the plantation.

Hàoyǔ was so detailed that part way through his lengthy notes, Maria wanted Hàoyǔ to skip to the punch line. "Just get to the point, Hàoyǔ. Where is the pendant?" Maria said out loud.

But, resolved to get tired and fall asleep, Maria slowed down and took her time, reading carefully.

When Hàoyǔ got to the burned house, he made notes about the placement of the giant boulder behind the house. She hadn't noticed this before. He included a small diagram of the house, with many dimensions, detailing the location of Leiya's furniture, including her bed and nightstand. Every fact he could remember, he recorded. It was typical Hàoyǔ, Maria noted.

She continued until she got to the description of Leiya's gruesome death. This was hard to read. By now, she was impressed with Kai and Leiya. She had been drawn in by their story; they were two amazing people who got what they didn't deserve.

Hàoyǔ's description of Leiya's persecution and death was poignant. Leiya was praying for everyone, out loud, by name. Including her persecutors. She prayed for their salvation and that God would show them one day the same grace she was experiencing right then. She barely reacted to the knife cuts, gave God the glory, and *thanked* Him.

Maria's heart skipped and she caught her breath. Her eyes filled with tears. She wanted to go back in time and meet Leiya, be her friend, learn from her about life, love, and God.

Maria wiped her eyes with her sleeve, but more tears were coming. She started sobbing.

She got up for a tissue. She raised her arms in the air and looked upwards, tears streaming, "God, who are you that you produce this kind of change in a person? Two years prior, Leiya was trying to follow the Tao but assumed it was impossible. Then she discovered that Jesus is the Tao, and she was changed. *Her death proved it!* I want this kind of faith, God. I want what Leiya had! I do, God."

Maria cried out loudly, "I'm serious, God. I want Leiya's kind of faith. I want my life to be in your hands, so much that I could give my life willingly to advance what you want. Change me, Lord!"

Her heart eventually settled, and she came back to the table. She continued reading. She made it to the page with the simple diagram locating the pendant. This page contrasted with the others; it was barely more than a triangle, whereas the other pages were loaded with text and detailed drawings.

She asked out loud, "Why Hàoyǔ? Why on this page can't you be a little more forthcoming?"

She knew the answer to the rhetorical question. If the notes fell into the wrong hands, they needed to be complex. A gravedigger, looking for a quick bit of gold, would get frustrated and give up.

In the upper right corner of the page was a circle and a north symbol. Just below the north arrow, inside the ring, was the number 360.

Maria thought it seemed odd that Hàoyǔ would have to make a notation to say something so obvious that a circle has 360 degrees to it.

The merry-go-round flashed in her mind, and the Chinese man telling her to remember that circles are *measured* by 360 degrees. *Measured*.

Maria's mind pondered that word. What is significant about the word measured?

All the measurements on the diagrams were in li for the large distances and bu for the short distances. And it was common knowledge what distances they were.

Curious, though, Maria grabbed her phone and looked up "Chinese *measurements* of distances, Ming dynasty."

One of the first pages that came up was on Wikipedia.

Maria gasped.

There it was! The Chinese li was infamously unstable over time. Even as late as 1930, the values changed again. This she knew.

What she didn't know, what shocked her, was that during some eras, the li was based on 360 bu *and* 300 bu. Hàoyǔ was indicating that he had used a li based on 360 bu.

Maria did the math quickly, certain she had found the answer to the length discrepancy. Surely the distance between the cross and the rock would have to be correct, based on a 360 bu.

Disappointment showed up again, however, like a sad-face clown at a birthday party. It wasn't a match. It was much closer, but not exact. The distance they had measured today was *still too long*.

Maria was frustrated. Out loud, she gave a long sigh and said, "What else is missing?"

She was off by 6.1 meters, or .011 li.

Not sleepy, she realized this jigsaw puzzle wasn't getting her any closer to sleep or an answer.

Maria's mind wandered back to Leiya. She had been an admirable woman in every respect. This story was about Leiya; even the town was named Leiya. The grave they were looking for was Leiya's.

Yet, the grave was the only point on the triangle related to Leiya. The other two points they hypothesized were Kai's crucifixion and a rock of no importance.

Maria felt there must be something else in the diagrams, two things that were Leiya's. She needed to close the gap by .011 li.

Leiya had been laid on a table near the cross so Kai would be forced to watch his wife die. Perhaps it was Maria's table they needed to use. Maria flipped back to the description of the persecution. In words, Hàoyǔ described how far the table was from Kai. He even said the table was centered on the cross, an important point because the cross' ground marker was laid out in the exact direction of the grave.

Maria translated the distance from the cross to Leiya's table. It was .06 li.

Maria was closing in on the answer. She had absorbed .06 of the .11 she needed to find.

She turned her attention to the point of the triangle near the boulder. Following the same line of thinking, she postulated that the point of the triangle must belong to Leiya.

She flipped to the house diagram.

She started closest to the boulder and did the math for some objects.

The corner of the house? Not very significant, she thought, but she measured it anyway. It was not enough.

The bed? That was Leiya's. But, no. It was too far.

It had to be between the corner of the house and the bed.

The nightstand? Not sure why, but… Yes! Perfect!

But why the nightstand?

Maria guessed that the jewelry must have been found where the nightstand was.

They were looking for the pendant made from the jewelry! It made sense that Hàoyǔ would choose that point as one of the triangle's three points.

Maria stepped away from the table. It was clear now. Why hadn't it clicked before? It was all about Leiya.
1. Triangle Point 1) Where Leiya died.
2. Triangle Point 2) Where Leiya's jewelry melted so it could be made into a pendant.
3. Triangle Point 3) Where Leiya's body and pendant were.

The triangle was about Leiya. Hàoyǔ must have known that if anything went wrong in verbally/physically handing down the grave site location, someone could figure it out from his written notes.

"Praise Jesus!" Maria said out loud. "Praise Jesus! Praise Jesus!"

She looked at her watch. It was 4:30. She texted Martin. "I think I have the three points of the triangle! Praise Jesus!"

Martin responded, "What?!! Hallelujah! Getting dressed. You at the cabin? Be right there."

When he arrived, Maria went through all the logic with him, pointing out the various pieces of information in the notes.

Then she went through all the math with him. He cross-checked everything on his phone.

"It seems to fit," he said. "I guess we will know shortly!"

"It's getting light out, Martin. Let's go treasure hunting!"

The project proved more complicated than they first thought, however. Only one side of the triangle was easy. The distance from Leiya's death site to the melted jewelry was only about 90 meters, traversing open ground. But the other two legs of the triangle were partially in the woods and as much as 500 meters each.

They started to measure with the 25-meter tape measure but quickly gave up, realizing they couldn't stay true to the correct angle; every 25 meters was another chance to get slightly off course.

"Martin, I think we need rope to do this accurately."

"Got it," Martin responded, "we sell nylon cord at the camp store. I'll be right back."

Turning Outward Dissolves The Hurt

Kai sat on a log around a small open fire a few feet away from Leiya's grave. It had become part of his evening ritual over the past few weeks. It was just the two of them, silent, except for the snapping of the fire.

Hàoyǔ had agreed to rebuild the plantation. Kai had the money to rebuild, and it seemed the right thing to do. The legacy of the plantation couldn't die with Leiya, Kai insisted. Hàoyǔ found a few workers who had fled to Ningde and paid them triple wages to return and take a chance on rebuilding.

Kai had to leave. Not only did he have to complete his work for God, but he could not let Leiya down. They had vowed to do His will together. She always intended to be here at the plantation while he was away. In some ways, Kai reasoned, it was still this way. She was here, in the ground, and she would always be here.

It was sad and lonely being left behind. In a way, he wished he had died on that cross; he would be rejoicing in heaven with the woman and Savior he loved.

But he knew… He had to keep going.

The second reason he had to leave was for the protection of Hàoyǔ and the workers. Eventually, it would be discovered that he survived, and evil would return.

223

This was his last night. He had accomplished what he needed before leaving. The plantation was in Hàoyǔ's capable hands, and the China pendant was in a secure place where it would only be found by someone God would later direct.

He had secured passage back to Japan. He planned to take some time to recuperate at the Onsen with his brother, the tea house, and God. He needed to bring the Japan pendant to his brother for safekeeping. And he needed some time to plan for the next country that would hear the Gospel.

Nobody knew what happened to Genghis. The last anyone saw was that he was still with Yìchén's men when they were told to leave. Kai logically assumed that Genghis had been killed, too, since a baby would be a burden to Yìchén. But, they never found Genghis' body; and this gave Kai hope that one day he would see his son again. Kai knew it was a remote chance, but he decided he was going to count on that hope.

Ju also had disappeared in the dispersion of the workers. Kai felt certain he would never see her again. He couldn't imagine why she would want to come back to this land after witnessing her sister's death and the destruction of everything her family had built.

Every night as he sat by Leiya's grave, he prayed for each of the men and women he had come to know at the plantation. Indeed, even during the day, he instinctively prayed for everyone as he remembered them. If they came to his mind, he prayed for them. Not a long prayer, but a petition before God. It quickly became a habit and a source of comfort; if he thought of someone, he prayed for them.

It gave him solace to converse all day with the Father. The loneliness wasn't as deep. He found His grace dissolved his hurt; his heart found peace by taking His love and turning it outward.

"I came to say goodbye," Hàoyǔ said from behind Kai. "We'll both be off early in the morning, and I didn't want to miss you. Is it okay to just have a few minutes with you tonight?"

"Of course, my friend. Please sit."

They sat in silence for a few minutes, staring into the fire.

"You're being left with a lot of responsibility," Kai said. "the business of the plantation and the ministry."

"These two blessings will always be my greatest responsibilities in life," Hàoyǔ promised.

"I intend to come back and visit from time to time. But it's best if people believe I died on that cross; we don't want to give Yìchén a reason to return. The scrolls will need to be copied and replaced as the writing grows old and becomes too hard to read. The legacy of the plantation needs to live long into the future. You've been here for two years, involved in the operation of the plantation and the Bible studies. You are ready, and you have the Holy Spirit. The Bible says that the Holy Spirit will teach you all things."

Hàoyǔ smiled. "Kai, I can tell you are a little nervous. You've already told me all these things. I am ready, my friend. God is with me. I don't want you to be concerned. God will grow all of this in His will and timing. I am confident. You will be pleased with what He has done when you come back to visit."

Hàoyǔ continued, "I will miss you, though, my friend. I want you to know how blessed I feel that God put us together. I was nothing more than a thug, destined for prison and hell. But your open resolve to share the love of Christ triggered something in me that night in Shanghai. I stood up to defend you, in strength not my own. And now I am ready to live the same open resolve to share Christ."

He hesitated briefly. "I want to thank you, Kai. You saved my life because you led me to the One with the power to save me. I will forever be grateful to you, my friend. I owe you my life."

Hàoyǔ choked on the final words. He stood up, trying to shake off the uncomfortable show of emotion. It was hard enough to say goodbye, but he had never properly thanked Kai. Hàoyǔ felt relieved to have put the words out there.

Kai stood up and put an arm on Hàoyǔ's shoulder.

"You are welcome, my brother. But it is you who deserves the thanks. You saved my life three times in the last two years."

Kai squeezed his shoulder to emphasize his last words.

"God has anointed our friendship, for His purposes, to glorify Him. God has kept us alive, and we can trust He will do so for as long as we are faithful and useful to Him. All glory to God in the Highest."

Generations of Anticipation

They laid the cord out in the open ground and measured it carefully. With both lines cut, they stretched them out in the general direction they needed. The theory was that the ropes would eventually meet at a point.

Going around trees was a challenge. Furthermore, the cord had some stretch to it. So, the ropes needed to meet with *equal* stretch; and, *the same stretch as when it was measured.*

They worked for hours. They carefully laid out each cord separately, working around trees, having to guess at the right angle. But when the ropes didn't meet at the end, they had to adjust one or both. This meant changing the angle, thereby changing the line around other trees.

Hu came out and assisted them. It was helpful to have more hands and eyes looking for the right angles.

They finally settled the two cords at a point and were convinced they had equal tension and adjustments for trees.

The location where the cords met was a considerable distance from where the grave was traditionally thought to be. It was far up into the hills, at least 100 meters above the little knoll where the grave location was presumed to have been.

From the flat ground, the slope traveled steeply over several knolls before reaching a small plateau and the start of another climb.

The place where the ropes met was not only far from where they expected; it was not a typical grave site. It was heavily wooded and rocky.

"This is the last place I expected," Hu said. "When we did previous measurements based on 300 bu/li, it led us to where we expected it to, which is why we never considered a different measurement system."

"But, that's also why when we brought in guys with metal detectors, we never found anything. The distances lined up with the flat ground down below. We never came way up here."

Hu pointed at the ground, "Even if we had looked at this place, we would have walked away! Nobody digs a grave in rocky ground like this; it's too much work compared to perfectly level sandy soil below. Hàoyǔ must have carried her mutilated body way up here. That would have been a significant challenge because he was probably doing this alone; Kai was recovering. Hàoyǔ's character is exemplary. Not only carrying her up here but digging a grave in this rocky terrain."

"I agree, dad," Martin added. "He must have known that he needed a place that would stand the test of time. It makes one wonder, too, did God lead him here? It's almost like a Moses scene here up on the side of this mountain. Leiya was an extraordinary woman who found her Savior and willingly laid down her life for the gospel's sake. From the description in Hàoyǔ's notes, she died in the full grace of the Lord. Hàoyǔ knew that. He must have sensed that the normal burial ground was not enough for this saint. It seems so perfect up here."

"It is perfect," Maria said, facing the valley, visible through the trees. "I can imagine that after Kai recovered, he would come up here to honor his wife, looking out over the valley, praying to God for the next chapter of His obedience."

"Yes," Hu said, "and imagine Kai leaving here. He was a sea captain who finally fell in love at age forty-five. His one true love. But God had kept him alive to do His work. And Kai left to do it. I can only imagine that kind of character in obedience. And thank God for Hàoyǔ, that he was such a historian, chronicling all of this for us."

"Well," Martin said, "what do you think? Should we call in the friends with the metal detectors? It seems like a sure bet we'll get some beeps here."

Maria looked at Martin and then at Hu.

Then all three turned their eyes to the ground, and smiled.

Maria said what they were all thinking, "Let's try the old-fashioned way first. God has been with us this far. We'll resort to the metal detector if we can't find it with a shovel."

It wasn't easy digging. Rocks needed to be cleared, some of them large. And tree roots had to be cut through with the spade.

But it wasn't long before the shovel hit metal.

It was a medium-sized, thick-cased, metal box. The box had a strong clasp and cover. It was further sealed with a thick coating of wax around the opening.

They carried it down the hill to Hu's house, knowing his wife would want to be there for the opening. When they had all gathered, and the wax seal was carved away, Maria held her breath as Hu raised his arms and poised to open up his ancestor's box.

Maria suddenly filled with emotion. Her breath stuttered audibly, and Martin closed in to hold her.

Hu looked up at Maria. He dropped his hands to wait.

Maria said, "I don't know why I am so emotional. I was crying last night when I was reading about Leiya's death. She was an extraordinary woman. And now we are about to open her box. I can't help it. I just wished I had known her."

Hu said, "Maria, your emotion is justified. She was extraordinary. But I want you to know that she lived an ordinary Christian life for those born from above. Her life isn't common because few find Jesus' narrow gate, and even fewer sacrifice as much as her, but for those who pursue Jesus as she did, they live in joy most will never know. We will all die one day, but to live in joy abundant for the remainder of our lives, and rest eternally in it, is a fabulous gift. You can be sure Leiya was rejoicing then and is still rejoicing!"

Maria cried harder in response to Hu's words. "I *know*. *That* made me cry last night. *That* is the emotion I feel right now."

She looked up at Melissa to find female acknowledgment of her tears, "I want what Leiya had, Melissa. And I am *not* ashamed to say it. I cried out to God in the early morning hours today. I begged God last night."

Melissa handed Maria a tissue. "Here, sweetheart." She then hugged Maria and held her tight.

Melissa whispered, "I assure you, with that attitude, you will know what Leiya knew. God gives grace to the humble. And He has already given it to you. You are going to be an amazing servant to Him. He has plans for you, my daughter."

Maria cried harder and hugged Melissa tighter. "Thank you, Melissa, I so appreciate what you have done for me. You have been kind to welcome me in, like a daughter. I love you. Thank you."

When Maria had settled, Hu said, "Let's give thanks and honor to our Lord before we open the box."

Hu prayed. Then Melissa prayed. Martin added his prayers, and then Maria felt the words coming from inside her spirit. She flowed with a prayer for God's will to move people closer to Him. She thanked Him for meeting her in her need, bringing people to her who took their time to teach her in a way she needed so that she could hear the truth about her loving Creator.

They opened their eyes after prayer and watched Hu get closer to the box. He carefully carved away a few remaining pieces of the thick wax seal.

When the latches were open, he looked up at everyone a last time. With his hands on the cover, he scanned each silent face, and without another word, he finally opened the box.

Inside, there was a large stack of papers.

They recognized the first pages as a copy of Hàoyǔ notes. Under that, in descending chronological order, were notes from other generations. The last notes were from the generation killed by persecution in the early 1800s.

Beneath the stack of papers was a thin wooden box. Inside that box was the long-anticipated pendant.

Hu picked up the pendant, looked at it briefly, and then placed it against his heart. Generations of anticipation spilled out uncontrollably. He started to cry and turned to his wife to hide his emotion. She held him as he sobbed.

The China pendant was finally found after four hundred years and eighteen generations of Oda ancestors who wanted to see it and send it back to Japan. Hu felt he was crying the emotion of not only himself but all his ancestors back to Kai and Leiya. He felt Kai's breath of relief after being released from the cross, the sadness of losing his wife, and the call to advance the gospel in the Asian world. He felt a resurgence of urgency to teach the Bible to Asians through the scriptures revealed in the scrolls.

Maria and Martin held hands as they watched Hu express the emotional relief that every Oda and every Japanese Christian would feel.

When he gathered himself, he thanked his wife, kissed her, and turned around. He looked at Martin, stepped forward, and hugged him.

He stepped away, still looking directly at Martin.

"Son, I am proud of the man you have become. You are kind, intelligent, ethical, and discerning. Most importantly, you are a man of God."

Hu's eyes started to mist again. "And I believe God has anointed you and Maria to take our pendant to Japan."

Hu gulped back emotion and continued, "There is something I haven't shared with you, my son. We discovered that there were more Oda Prophecies, back at the Onsen in Japan. Oda Nobumasa had left prophecies regarding someone who would be anointed to help bring the message of Christ to Japan. The prophecy was held closely by the generations in Japan; nobody knew but a single person within each generation. And there was no fulfillment until this generation.

"A 'foreign fish' had been prophesied to come to the Onsen, find the message of Christ, reject it, live through all the soils of the parable of the sower, and finally write a book about his long slow journey to accepting the Spirit of Adoption.

"This has happened. God called an American to fulfill the prophecy made through Nobumasa, the originator of the Tea Room Scrolls. His name is Isaiah. As prophesied, he was reticent to accept Christ but finally did so at the age of fifty and moved to the Oda Onsen. Also, as predicted, he wrote a book about his faith journey, a slow brewing journey that parallels the Japanese as a people. Your mom and I have read it: Slow Brewing Tea. He is now married to Nori Oda. I've been in touch with them recently. They knew Kai was Nobumasa's youngest brother but virtually nothing else. They didn't know about the plantation, the pendants, and Kai's travels to spread tearooms throughout Asia. They are searching at the Onsen for the Japanese pendant now.

Hu continued, "We will call Nori and Isaiah immediately with this news. But my question to you both: do you feel called to bring this pendant to Japan? And if not, would you please pray about it?"

Martin looked at his dad, then his mom. Finally, he looked at Maria. Still looking into Maria's eyes to make sure she was with him, he said,

"Dad, Maria and I have already discussed this. We believe God has called both of us."

Maria snuggled in close to Martin. "Hu and Melissa, with your blessing, we will carry the pendant to Japan and let God rule our next calling from there. All glory to God! Praise Jesus!"

A Letter to The Messenger

1817 by the pen of Samuel Oda

I'm writing this because our region is again facing great persecution against Christians. The information herein would usually be communicated to our family members when they are old enough to take responsibility.

With our family traditions at high risk of being thwarted by unspeakable evil, we opened the box in Leiya's grave to put this letter and two hundred years of family diaries. Please know that we resealed this box with our blessings and prayers to the one who eventually finds it. We have complete faith God will lead an anointed one to this pendant and bring it back to Japan in His timing for the greater advancement of the gospel in Japan. May His will be done on earth as it is in heaven.

The Tea Room Scrolls method of teaching the Bible has been a part of our heritage since Kai Oda built the tearoom on this plantation. Following the first persecution at the plantation when Leiya's house burned, Kai made eight pendants, each with a specific location where the Bible would be taught via the Tea Room Scrolls. Eventually, in

God's timing, all of the pendants would be reunited at the Oda family mountain in Japan. This box contains the pendant left in China.

Generations of our family have prayed over this pendant, starting with Kai and Leiya themselves. A particular focus of our prayers relates to a revelation God gave our family (as recorded in the notes from 1687). God revealed to our family that an anointed woman would be the one to find this pendant. This woman would have found faith at this plantation and would carry the same resolve and unwavering faith as Leiya. The dream happened 50 years after Leiya was killed and was confirmed in other revelations.

If the dream was correct, and it is a woman finding this letter, welcome to our family. We believe you are like a daughter to Leiya. You share the same disposition, determination, and love for Jesus Christ as Leiya. You are essential to the Oda legacy as God reveals Himself to the Japanese. And while your faith may be new, we believe you will grow to know a faith so strong that you will experience the Kingdom of God as revealed in His grace and the beatitudes of Jesus Christ.

The pendant and this letter must be brought to Oda Onsen in Japan, located in the mountains outside Aomori. The Holy Spirit wouldn't have led you to the pendant if this task were impossible. You are encouraged to trust the God who blessed you with this anointing.

Just like the tea leaves of our family, your faith will be seasoned by fire. Your experiences may seem unbearable at times. Trials, even persecution, sometimes accompany great faith and anointing. Without such faith, this pendant will never reach its destination, nor will you endure to the end. "But the one who endures to the end will be saved." Mat 24:13

Members of our family have been praying for you since 1687. We do not know what will happen once all the pendants have made it to Japan. We know that *you* have been led to *this* pendant, and you have the blessing and responsibility of taking it to the tearoom where Nobumasa birthed the original Japanese method of studying the Bible, the Tea Room Scrolls.

Maybe this will be the last pendant to make the trip to Oda Onsen; maybe there are still more to make the journey. What matters to you at present is that this pendant, our family's pendant, China's pendant, and now your pendant, is taken home by you.

Blessings for your travels. God has anointed the wind in your sails. He initiated Japan's awakening in the 1500s, advanced His will through Nobumasa, Kai, Leiya, every generation of Oda on this plantation, and He will advance His will through you. Rest assured, He is faithful to complete what He starts.

Hallelujah to the Lamb!